Eddie's Back

Russell R Vitrano

Published by Russell R Vitrano, 2024.

EDDIE'S BACK

First edition. July 4, 2024.

ISBN: 979-8224786015

Written by Russell R Vitrano.

Deep Gratitude to my Devoted parents, Vincent and Eleanor Vitrano. Also to JAN my life Partner.

This Book is Dedicated to ALL Baby boomers, Especially the ones I grew up with. Rain Snow or Shine the Outdoors was our unlimited Playground.

We walked to and from school, playing games building our Imagination. We arrived home an hour or two later to an unlocked front door.

Also a very special thanks to ALL Veterans, serving or have served. Protecting and keeping America FREE.

Because of ALL mentioned - I was driven to write this book. Thank You .... GOD BLESS AMERICA

CHAPTER 1 - MILWAUKEE WISCONSIN - 1961

(B LACK AND WHITE)
The Crawford's, family of four watch intently as their small television flickers with a grainy black and white image of newly elected President John F Kennedy. "And so my fellow Americans. Ask not what your country can do for you. Ask what you can do for your country." The intensity of his words hang over the modest living room. 38 year old Wayne Crawford instinctively adjusts his tie, Jane Crawford age 37, nervously brushes the smooth strands of her perfectly coifed hair back from her flushed cheeks. With a meaningful glance at his sons Wally and Chip. Wayne pushes up from his easy chair, buttons his suit jacket, walks to the 21 inch television, turns it off. "Dad" blurts out 16 year old Wally. "Eddie got a job at Al's gas station. Can I drive the Vespa to see him"? Wayne's eyes open wide. "Al's a good man. A Korean war hero. Eddie's in good hands. He will learn and experience many things working with Al Dawson". "Can I go too dad, can I can I". Chimed in his 11 year old brother Chip. Wayne Smiles, "Okay Wally take Chip with you. Have Eddie fill the tank. Buy a few soda's with the change. Wayne flips a Ben Franklin silver half dollar towards Wally. Chip intercepts it. " Gee thanks dad". "Boy's be careful". Jane warns with motherly concern. "Oklahoma Avenue is busy this time of day. Chip tuck in your shirt, comb your hair". "Aw - mom". Chip protests runs to the door. "Boys dinners at 6 don't be late".

Wally kick starts the Vespa. Revs the 50cc engine. Wee Wee. Chip hops on, hangs on to Wally he turns on his AM transistor radio. (MUSIC UP) The Wolf man plays early rock and roll music. The vespa cruises the city streets. The boys wave to girls playing hopscotch on the sidewalk. They wave to well dressed people walking their dogs, talking to their neighbors. They cruise by kids running playing kick the can. The wind blows through their hair as the vespa takes a sharp right turn. Two girls with hula hoops wave at Wally and Chip. The Vespa cruises by fine manicured lawns white picket fences. They wave at children playing catch with their dad on the sidewalk. Slow driving smiling motorists, driving big American made cars, covered in chrome wave at the wind blown boys.

The smiling boys, arrive at Al's triangle gas station. A sign reads REGULAR Gas 25.9 - ETHEL Gas 29.9. A man dressed in brown pants tucked in brown shirt,
thoroughly cleans the windows of a customers car.
Beads of sweat form on his forehead. This is 30 year old Al Dawson Korean war hero. Rough - Handsome a John Wayne type. He is sole owner of Al's triangle gas station.
Al tips his cap. "Ma'am your oil is fine. The left rear tire needs air. I'll have Eddie fill it. The gas comes to $3.75. "She smiles, hands Al a $5 bill. He gives her change and green stamps. "Thank you, we appreciate your business. Eddie fill her left rear tire 35 lbs. pressure, check the others". A young man runs to the customers car. This is 15 year old Eddie Harper, tall clean cut blond wavy hair. Eddie proudly wears tarnished brown work clothes, two rags hang out of his pockets. " I'm on it Al, sir". Eddie dances around the car, fills the tires checks his air gauge. Eddie struts to the drivers open window, pulls a rag from his pocket, wipes his hands, smiles. "Ms. your tires are good as new". She smiles. "Thank you Eddie, see you soon". Eddie waves. "Take care now, see you next week".
The 50cc vespa putts, Wally pulls up to Eddie's pump. Eddie laughs. "Ha Crawford, is this what I think it is? A Japanese toy bicycle". Chip hops off the vespa. "Knock it off Eddie". Eddie laughing points. "Hey squirt this is a girls bike". Wally kicks the kickstand. "Oh yeah at least we have one". Chip yells. "Yeah where's yours"? Eddie smiles as he struts around the small vespa. "Don't worry small fry.

Some day one day - You will see me cruising the streets of Milwaukee, on my American made Harley Davidson". Eddie holds both arms up, pretending to ride a chopper. "Oh yeah I'll look just like James Dean. All the girls will just have to wait in line". Wally laughs. "Eddie you're a dreamer"! Eddie spins. "We will see gents. My dad works at Harley. He will get me a Daddy-O deal". They laugh.

Al Dawson walks to the gas pump. "Harper quit the chit chat, Take care of the Crawford's. I'll be in the garage, helping Leroy with that brake job". Eddie straightens up. "Can I help you gentlemen"? Al shakes his head walking towards his gas garage. Chip says. "Fill it up Eddie - Make it snappy". Eddie looks towards the garage. "Easy small fry, don't get your underwear bunched in a binder now". Wally laughs. Eddie fills the vespa. Checks the oil, tire pressure. "Wow this toy took a whole 23 cents".

Vroom Vroom - A souped up yellow 1932 ford coupe, license plate FEB - 359. Rumbles onto the gas station lot. Everyone turns and looks! Chip points. "Look Wally neat race car". "Chip that's Don Miller, He has the fastest car in town". A smiling well built handsome 19 year old man, neatly combed hair exits the yellow ford coupe. Don Miller wears blue jeans, white tee shirt. A pack of smokes is rolled into his short sleeves.

Eddie pulls a rag, wipes his hands, "Don my man, how's it hanging"? "Super Harper just super. Hey Wally, how's track going"? "Great Don, we should make it to the state meet in Madison". "That's great. Did I ever tell you guys? Back in 58 I made it to state". Don winds up spins his 180 lb body. Pretends to throw a shot put. Eddie shakes his head. "Yeah yeah Don - you told us that story a million times".

Don stares at his hot rod. "Eddie fill it with ethel. Check the oil. We have to adjust the valves". Don lights a cigarette. Eddie lifts the hood. "The valves Don? My man what's up"? Don takes a drag from his cigarette. "Ah there's a new muscle car cruising town looking for me". Wally points at the yellow coupe. "You'll cream him Don. You always do. That yellow bomb beats all". Eddie smiles. "Hell yeah! They never learn". Eddie, Wally, Don slap five. Chip smiles. Don crushes his cigarette. "Yeah guys as long as they line up. I'll shut them down". Chip points. "Wow look cool car".

A sparkling white 1961 Corvette Stingray. Driven by a stunning blonde crawls up to a gas pump. This is Barb Midway 19 beautiful. Don looks - gasps'. "Wow guys, look at that hot stuff coming out of Detroit these days". Eddie looks grins, covers his mouth. "Forget the car man, check out that hot dame". Don turns whispers. "Down Boy easy, control now all business". Eddie looks towards Al's Garage. He struts to the white spic and span 61 Corvette. "Beautiful lady Al's station at your service. My name is Eddie Harper. All the girls call me Eddie. How may I help you on this fine beautiful afternoon"?

Barb pulls out her compact. Applies more red lipstick. Stares into the mirror. "3 dollars regular gas". Check my motor. When I floor it, I hear a funny noise". "Yes doll Eddie at your service". Eddie lifts the hood. Winks at the guys. Bites his wrist. Don flicks his cigarette, confidently walks to the Blonde bombshell.

"Excuse me miss, I know why you hear that ping sound when you rev your engine". Barb drops her mirror into her fancy purse. "Yeah, you know. You work here"? Eddie slams the hood. "This is Don Miller, fastest car in town. He's tuned cars all his life. Don knows all". Wally jogs to the corvette. You never heard of thee Don Miller. Don never lost a race". Barb brushes her long blonde hair. "Ah Yeah - I think I heard of him".

Barb drops her brush. "Oh! you're the guy. He's looking for". Eddie screams. "What - who's looking for Don"? Barb picks up her fancy hair brush, points west, "I was cruising 27th street. This guy wearing a white cowboy hat, driving a black 57 Chevy, pulls next to me at the light. He revs his car, then he asks me. Where can I find this Miller guy? He drives a piss yellow tin can"? Don lights a cigarette, inhales a long drag. "Then he says, tell him there's a new sheriff in town. I aim to blow his ass off the road. Then he patched out. Wow - I just love it when guys lay rubber. Man his car was bitchen fast".

Eddie looks at Don. "Don my man. Those 57 Chevy's are tuff. You are right boss. We better adjust your valves. I'll get Leroy to help". Don takes a long drag. Stares at his yellow car. Chip runs to the corvette. "Wow miss, he patched out. Did the tires smoke? Was his cowboy hat like the one the lone ranger wears"? Don waves his arms. "Guys lay off the dame. She just came in for some gas".

Don flicks his cigarette, looks at Barb. "Doll your car pings because you buy regular gas". Barb's finger twirls her long blonde hair. "Well yeah! (pause) I have to put gas in the car. (pause) Don't I"? The guys look at each other. Don lifts the corvette's hood. "Look you drive a four barrel carburetor with 230 horsepower. Don't ask for regular gas. Ask for Ethel. It's a higher octane gas". Barb raises here perfectly shaped eyebrows. "Ethel"? Don points to the gas sign. "Ethel gas the premium stuff". Barb looks, "I have to buy the more expensive gas"? Eddie smiles. "Expensive gas for the expensive lady". Everyone laughs, Chip looks.

Don twists the gas cap off the glowing white corvette stingray. "Harper fill this to the brim with ethel, She will lay rubber all around town". Laughter - Eddie grabs the silver gas nozzle, gently places it into the corvette gas tank. Chips eyes are fixed on Eddie, as he hops to the front checks the oil and water. Eddie crawls like a cheetah around the corvette, checks the air pressure in all tires. He pulls a rag from his back pocket wipes the corvettes windows, in perfect timing the gas pump clicks shuts off. Eddie gently removes the gas nozzle, smiles. "Ten gallons 3 dollars please".

Barb digs into her fancy purse, hands Eddie a crisp 10 dollar bill and 3 singles. "Keep the change". Don, Wally, Chip's mouths drop. Eddie stuffs the crisp 10 dollar bill in his shirt. Barb plays with her bangs. "Oh one more thing, her finely manicured red nails point to the hood, of the beautiful white corvette. "That scratch, where can I get it fixed"?

Eddie, Don and Wally stare at the waxed shimmering hood. They bend to get eye level. Eddie smirks, "Scratch where"? Barb points. "Look it's in the middle". Wally's eye ball is one inch above the hood. "I think I see it, look there guys". Eddie gently wipes a small area. "Oh that small little thing"? Barb points. "Can you fix it? It's not the size that matters". Eddie turns around looks at the guys. His face is disheveled holding in a laugh.

Eddie rubs his chin, faces Barb. "Hmm I understand about the size, let me think". Eddie scratches his head. Raises his finger. "I got it". Eddie slaps Don's back. "Don here is very good at bodywork"! He winks at Wally. Barb's eyes open wide. "Don can you fix that scratch for me"? Don touches the hood. "Sure a little bondo and some touch up paint will do the trick". She hands Don a slip of paper. "Cool here's my number. I'm Barb, I'll be expecting your call". Barb fixes her hair in her rear view mirror, smiles drives off.

Eddie turns twists and shouts. "Miller! you lucky son of a bitch". Wally buts in. "Don when are you going to call her". Eddie grabs Don's white t shirt, "Miller you better call her. If you don't I will. That is one fine looking babe". Don pulls away from Eddie's grip. "Guys what the big deal. She just wants her scratch fixed". "Scratch fixed"? Eddie moves his fingers 3 inches apart. "She also said, It's not the (size) that matters"! Eddie, Wally, Don explode in crazy laughter. Chip looks.

Al Dawson wipes his hands with a brown rag - jogs towards the gas pumps. "Eddie what's going on out here"? "Oh not much Mr. Dawson". Eddie winks. "Don just picked up some extra bodywork"! Boys laugh slap five. Chip looks. Al Dawson hands on hips shakes his head. "She's out of your league men. That's Barb Midway. Her father Ben owns Jiffy Trucking. Largest trucking firm east of the Mississippi. They live in a mansion off Lake Shore Drive". Eddie looks at Don. "Wow that is one rich broad".

Al looks. A sputtering steaming old car crawls up to the gas pump. Driven by a gray haired aging woman. Her wide eyed grand daughter sits in the passenger seat. Al smiles waves. "Hello Mrs. Brown, Hi Connie". "Hi Mr. Dawson". "Mrs. Brown you're running hot". "Oh my, Al it started steaming a while ago. Connie and I were at Bay view Park. What's wrong with my car Al"? " Let's see here". Al rag in hand slowly opens the hood. A dense fog escapes. "Wow! Chip yells. The boys move closer. Al extends both arms. "Careful men". Al wipes the radiator cap.

Al (Looks) shakes his head. He turns towards his garage.

"Hey Leroy take a look at this". A smiling stocky man, late twenties, wearing greasy brown work cloths, jogs out of Al's garage. This is Leroy Johnson. Al's right hand man. Leroy nods to everyone. He tips his 1957 world series champion Milwaukee Braves cap to Mrs. Brown. Leroy fans away the steam - puffs his cigar. "Oh yeah, I've seen this a hundred times. A car with over 70.000 miles". Al Dawson shakes his head. "It's the water pump". "Yes boss that's what I say". Don Miller grabs a rag, shakes the radiator fan. "For sure it's the pump. I've seen these things blow at 40,000 miles". Don grabs Leroy's flashlight, points. "And lookey there Al. She ran so hot the damn engine block cracked".

Mrs. Brown with concern in her voice. "Oh my, Al can you fix it"? Al rag in hand, wipes his hands as he slowly walks over to Mrs. Brown's window. "I'm sorry Mrs. Brown. You need a whole new engine, radiator, water pump, hoses, battery and more". Mrs. Brown cries. "Why what happened"? "You see ma'am, the water pump blew then all the water leaked out of the radiator. With no coolant everything under the hood melted. It all has to be replaced. This is a major job".

Tears run down Mrs. Brown's face. Connie looks at her grandmother, she cries. Chip looks, cries. Mrs. Brown wipes her tears. "My dear is it expensive Al? Since Sam died things are tight, with the bills and all". Mrs. Brown breaks down, six year old Connie balls. Eddie, Don, Wally hang their heads. Al (stops) looks - stares at Leroy! Leroy grabs a wrench from his back pocket. "Now just wait a minute here. No reason for anyone to get upset. It's a new decade and we have a new president". Leroy puffs on his cigar.

"Let me take a closer look at this". Leroy whistles (Sweet Georgia Brown). He turns a few bolts spins a few screws, bends a few hoses, fans the engine with his ball cap. "That should do it. Eddie fill Mrs. Browns radiator with water". Everyone looks! Al smiles. "Go ahead Eddie - Let's go. I'm sure Connie and Mrs. Brown have better things to do then hang around here".

Eddie fills the radiator to the brim. Leroy puffs his cigar. "Okay Mrs. Brown fire your car up". The car purrs like a kitten. Don Miller LOOKS - questions. "Good as new? Leroy what the hell did you do"? Al winks at Leroy.. Mrs. Brown smiles. "Oh Leroy you're an (Angel)". Leroy smiles, his pearl white teeth glisten, laughs.

Al grabs the clean silver handle of his gas pump, twists her gas cap. Mrs. Brown yells. "No Al, I cant afford gas today". Al smiles. "This tank's on me". Eddie cleans her windows. six year old Connie reaches out the window, tugs on Al's shirt. "Mr. Dawson - when I grow up I want to be just like you". "What's that kid? A grease monkey". Everyone laughs. Al winks at Mrs. Brown. "No silly - I want to be a war hero like you. Grandma told me, you have lots of medals, even the purple heart". "A war hero, you want to carry a gun"? Al winks at Mrs. Brown. He looks into Connie's eyes. "That's good kid. Follow your dreams. Make your dreams come true Connie".

Six year old Connie's eyes open wide. "Yes sir I will". Eddie hands her green stamps. "Mrs. Brown - you have a lovely grand daughter". Mrs. Brown smiles. "Thank you gentlemen, God Bless". Tears in her eyes Mrs. Brown and Connie drive off.

Chip scratches his head. "Hey Wally - do they let girls in the Army"? "Ah - I guess so. They can be a nurse or secretary, something like that". Al Dawson shines his gas pumps. "Men when I was struggling, starting Al's triangle service station. Sam Brown helped me many times. As my father used to say. Help people, because someday when you need help. Hopefully someone will help you. Remember that men - it Evens out". Leroy flips his cigar. "Amen Al - my granddaddy Henry Johnson said to me. Leroy what goes around comes around".

Leroy looks to the blue sky. "I miss Sam Brown - He always offered a helping hand. A small loan that turned into a gift. Box seat tickets to a Brave game. A cup of coffee a cold soda - Damn"!

Chip tugs on Al Dawson's shirt. "Mr. Dawson do you have a soda machine"? "I sure do son. Men let's go inside. Drinks on me". Everyone cheers, as they walk inside Al's gas station. Chip's eyes open wide as he looks at 2 rooms. In the larger room a car rests up on the rack, it's four tires are removed. Tools, rags, new tires, oil cans, compliment the work room. The smaller room is Al's office. A black and white television plays - I Love Lucy. Al's manual cash register, a candy machine, a red vertical coke machine, and World War II posters of Normandy and General Mac Arthur cover the walls of the entire establishment.

Chip holds up two silver dimes. "Mr. Al my dad gave me and Wally 10 cents each for a soda - See"! Al puts his arm around Chip. "Son give that money to your dad. Tell Wayne I said hello, Semper fi, and (Save the red Eagle)". "Yes sir".

"Ah - what does save the red eagle mean"? The room stops. Everyone looks at Al. "That's a secret. I hope you men will never have to experience". Eddie's eyes open wide. Al punches a few keys, the cash register flies open. "Let's see six thirsty men here". Al grabs six silver dimes. "Okay men pick your poison". They line up, pull an 8 oz. bottle out. The bottle opener attached to the machine. A few caps fall on the floor.

Eddie turns the channel on the 16 inch television. "Wow - check it out. Elvis the king". Elvis Presley wears black slacks white socks a shiny jacket. He holds the microphone stand in his left hand. His guitar in right hand as his knees and hips swivel and shake. He jerks and twists across the entire long stage in a few seconds, without missing a lyric. The predominantly female audience goes wild. They scream, dance, fight to get on stage. Al points. "I remember that! That was Pan Pacific auditorium in LA - October 28, 1957. I was there, wow what a show Elvis put on. The place was packed over 9,000 screaming fans". Wally reacts. "You saw Elvis live! - I mean in person". The room looks at Al.

Al sits on cases of 8 oz. soda bottles. He glances at the television. "Damn - it was over 3 years ago. I remember it like it was yesterday. I was dressed in my full military uniform, so they let me up front. There were dames all around me going crazy. Bumping into me - rubbing against me. Hell I didn't mind - no not one bit". "Laughter" - Eddie, Wally spit their soda. Leroy lights a cigar. "Tell us more Al. Tell us about Elvis before he put down his mean guitar".

"Well - I was on leave in full uniform, standing touching the stage. In between songs, Elvis shook my hand then winked. As if to say - I'll be in uniform soon". Al points at Elvis rocking out on the black and white television. " Guess what men. Five months later Elvis enters the army. Then the plane crash February 3, 1959". Al points at Don's yellow car. "Don's license plate, Feb-359. Many say that's the day the music died".

Leroy pushes close to the television. He quickly moves the rabbit ears. Leroy stares - Elvis twists, shakes and bakes. Eddie moves towards Al. "Elvis shook your hand? Come on Al - why didn't you tell us that before"? Al smiles, "I didn't think it was that big of a deal, I've shaken lots of hands". Al points to his world war II posters on the wall. "General MacArthur, President Eisenhower".

Chip scratches his head. "Hey Wally - I thought Elvis was a movie star"? The room explodes in Laughter. "He is. Before Elvis was in the movies, He made records. He played guitar, sang and danced on stage - look". Leroy's face is flush against the television screen. Eddie grabs Leroy's shoulder. "Leroy step aside. Let the youngster see the real Elvis. The man that took rock and roll to the next level. Check it out - Elvis the pelvis".

Leroy turns away from the screen. His eyes are the size of golf balls. Leroy huffs and puffs, grabs a paper towel, wipes the sweat off his forehead. Flops onto an easy chair, chugs his root beer. "My Lord - I never seen a man shake, twist and shout like that - without missing a beat on his guitar". Leroy jumps up - he shakes and bakes, twists and shouts. "Especially - A white man"! The room explodes in Laughter. Leroy dances. More laughter. Leroy shakes, slaps five. Al points to the round black and white clock on the wall. "Men it's 5 o'clock quitting time.

Eddie stick around, Don use the garage, adjust your valves. Have Leroy set the timing. He'll show you and Eddie a trick or two". Don shakes Al's greasy hand. "Thanks Al". "Eddie you and Leroy lock up. If you need me I'll be across the street at Leo's gin mill. Enjoying a shot and cold beer". Leroy smiles. "Boss I'll join you later. A cold tapper of PBR sounds mighty fine". Wally jumps on the Vespa. "Chip let's go. Mon said dinners at 6".

DISSOLVE TO: SEPTEMBER 13, 1962

CHAPTER 2 - LET'S GO TO THE MOON

Early morning, the smell of sizzling bacon and percolating coffee fills the air. Toast pops up as Jane Crawford wearing an apron cracks eggs that sizzle in her frying pan. Wayne Crawford walks into the kitchen, sporting a business suit holding the rolled morning newspaper. "Good morning Jane". "Good morning dear".

Knock Knock - Eddie Harper stands outside. Wayne nods. Eddie wearing a letter sweater opens the door. His shirt is tucked into his pressed dress pants. "Good morning Eddie". "Good morning Mr. Crawford". Jane pours orange juice. "Hello Eddie". "A very good morning to you Mrs. Crawford. Wow did you just return from the beauty parlor? Your hair looks stunning this fine early morning". Jane smiles, touches her hair. "Thanks Eddie but no. I go to the beauty parlor on Saturdays". Eddie turns to Mr. Crawford. "Mr. Crawford your suit. Is that the same style Cary Grant wears"? Wayne and Jane make eye contact. Wayne adjusts his tie. "I don't think so. I buy my suits off the rack on Mitchell street". Jane holds the coffee pot. "Eddie you're early this morning". "Yes ma'am my workout went quick today. I believe I shattered the four minute mile". Jane makes eye contact with her husband as she pours coffee. "Eddie would you like to join us"? "Oh Mrs. Crawford, I hear you are a great cook. It would be an honor". Jane turns away, holds in a laugh.

Wayne and Eddie sit at a perfectly set kitchen table. Wayne opens his newspaper. Wally and Chip enter. Their hair is combed. Their collard shirts are tucked in. Wally wears his letter sweater. Jane cracks two eggs, adds them to the sizzling frying pan. Wayne looks up. "Good morning boys". "Hi Mom hi dad". Chip looks, Eddie? "Yes, good morning Wallace and how is little Chipper this morning"? "Why are you here Eddie? Free food". Wayne pushes his open newspaper down. "Chip behave! It's good to have friends, you might need them someday. Don't you agree"? Chip hangs his head. "I ah, I guess so sir, sorry Eddie". Wally and Chip sit. Jane holds her frying pan as she walks to the table. She scoops her spatula as she fills five plates with sunny side up eggs and sizzling bacon. A plate of hot buttered toast rests at the center of the table. The aroma from the hot crisp bacon fills the kitchen.

Wayne rests his newspaper on the table. "What's going on at school boys"? Chip holds his glass of milk. A white mustache has formed on his upper lip. "Same old stuff dad". Wayne rolls his newspaper. "What about you Wally" "Mr. Rife is teaching us that new math. I don't understand why we have to learn that junk anyway". Wayne picks up his newspaper. "Boys that new math is important. I was just reading about President Kennedy's speech at Rice University". Jane pours coffee. "What about the speech dear"?

" President Kennedy wants to put on man on the moon, before this decade is over". Everyone stops eating. Chip wipes his mustache. "Wow dad just like the comic books". Eddie laughs. "No way - the moon is to far away". Wally grabs more toast. "Will that happen in our life dad"? Wayne shakes his head. This president wants to do it before 1970, that's less than 8 years"! Jane sips on her hot black coffee. "I like this new president. He has so many new ideas". Wayne grabs his coffee cup. "I agree, to put a man on the moon, then return him to earth! Wow - what would the Russians think". Chip circles his fork around his food. "I wonder if Martians life on the moon"? Eddie wipes his mouth. "Heck no! Martians live on Mars. If they live on the moon, they are Moonchens". Everyone chuckles.

Wayne rest his cup on its saucer. Adjusts his tie. "Boys just think 70 years ago 1892 people did not drive cars. Horses were used. Now we have a President that wants to put a man on the moon before 1970. Wow what an accomplishment"! Chip asks. "Dad will he be president in 1970"? Wally holds his orange juice. "No Chip. We learned in history class that a president can only hold office for 8 straight years max". Eddie looks. "So 1968 is president Kennedy's last year". Wayne nods. "I'm sure JFK wants to get to the moon before 1968. What drive what goals are new president has". Wayne looks at his watch. Stands kisses Jane. "Time for work". Jane looks at the round clock on the wall. "Boys don't be late for school".

Eddie stands. "Mrs. Crawford, thank you - outstanding succulent breakfast. Mr. Crawford thank you for the insightful current events you shared with us this morning. It was very enlightening and educational". Wayne makes eye contact with Jane. "Your welcome Eddie. Boys study that new math. With our new president, next century year 2000, you might live on the moon. Have a great day at school". They smile, walk out the door. Jane smiles clears the kitchen table.

DISSOLVE TO APRIL 1963

CHAPTER 3 - MEET BULLY BUTCH DAVIS

Eddie, Wally, Chip carry books, walk to school. The aroma of freshly cut green lawns fills the crisp morning spring air. White picket fences line the streets. Large chrome filled American made cars slowly drive by, wave at Eddie. Eddie pulls his transistor radio out of his top pocket of his neatly pressed collard shirt. He raises the antenna, spins the knob. Doo-Op music plays. "Damn that's sad - it's a crying shame. Wally looks. "What's that Eddie"? "Buddy Holley, Richie Valence - The Big Bopper die in that plane crash.

Chip looks up. "Wally is that the plane crash, that Mr. Dawson always talks about"? "Yeah Chip - February 3, 1959. Many people believe that's the day the music died. Especially Don and Al". "Don the guy with the yellow race car"? "Yeah Chip - Don's license plate. Feb-359. The day of the crash. It's strange how Don got those numbers".

Eddie kicks a stone. "Now we listen to this Doo-Op stuff". Wally looks across the street. "I think it sounds pretty good Eddie". "Ah it's okay, But it's not the same man". Chip looks up. "Same as what"? Eddie shakes his hips. "Same as when Elvis sang (Ready Teddy) and (Hound Dog) on the Ed Sullivan show back in 56. Man that was downtown". Eddie smiles. "My parents almost had a cow". Everyone laughs.

Eddie looks across the street. A group of neatly dressed girls walk to school. "Hey Wally who are you taking to prom"? Wally combs his hair. "Mary Rogers, who are you taking"? Eddie points across the street. "Hey hey - Heck so many dames want to go with me. I haven't made my mind up yet". Chip throws a stone. "Yuck" - Eddie grabs Chip behind his neck. "Hey squirt someday you'll like girls". Wally pushes Eddie. "Hey Casanova it's next month. The clock is ticking". "Easy sam easy, I know! Miller is driving us. "It's going to be a blast". Chip looks up. "Wally why is Don driving you guys to prom"? "Because 2 years ago Eddie helped Don adjust his valves. Then Don creamed that black 57 Chevy". Chip yells. "Oh I remember, the lone ranger guy in the cowboy hat". Eddie laughs. "Hell yeah, after that beat down. Don promised he would drive me and my friends to my senior prom".

Chip moves his books to his left arm. "Wow you guys, Don has so many cool cars. I wonder which one he will take"? Eddie skips a stone. "Beats me little guy". Chip turns right. "I'll see you guys later".

Chip approaches Trowbridge grade school. In the distance he sees 3 taller boys blocking the side walk. Chip crosses Delaware Avenue. The older boys cross, block Chip's path. The oldest boy is Butch Davis 12 years old chubby, tall for his age. Butch grabs Chips collar, pulls Chip against him. "Not so fast squirt - Give me your lunch money". Chip looks down. "Ah I - I don't have any money today". With his free hand Butch makes a fist. "Don't lie small fry. Do you want to go to school with your teeth in your back pocket"? His buddies laugh.

Chip pulls a silver Washington quarter from his pocket. Butch grabs the coin. "That's all, if you're lying to me Crawford - I'll pound you". Butch punches Chip's school books to the ground, papers fly. Tears run down Chips face. Chip pulls his 4 pockets out. A plastic 4 inch comb hits the pavement. "See Butch, that's all my lunch money". Butch steps on the comb, rubs it into the sidewalk. His buddies kick Chip's books to the gutter, "You're lucky today Chippy boy. Next time I'll give you a knuckle sandwich". Butch pushes Chip into the gutter. He and his cronies laugh jog away.

Eddie and Wally enter Bay view High school. The hallways are filled with well dressed students. They enter home room 222. The 12th grade students mingle talk in small groups. Girls wear long dresses and styled hair. Boys collared shirts tucked into pressed pants. A few guys horse around, talk about pro wrestler Dick the Bruiser on TV last night. Cheerleaders yell, jump practice their cheers.

BELL RINGS! A well dressed teacher, Miss Landers walks in. All students quickly move to their seats. A respectful silence hovers over the room. Miss Landers stares at the red white and blue flag. "Students please stand for the pledge of allegiance". All students rise, place their right hand on their heart. With total concentration and undivided attention, they stare at the American flag that hangs in the front of room 222 everyday. "I pledge allegiance to the flag of the United States of America and to the republic for which it stands one nation (under God) invisible with liberty and justice for all".

CHAPTER 4 - DON CALLS BARB MIDWAY

APRIL 1963

Don Miller in his yellow 1932 souped up ford coupe, cruises 27th street. Don downshifts and turns into Leon's Custard Drive Inn. The 1932 coupe rumbles, Don parks. A smiling attractive 17 year car hop skates to Don's car. Don opens his door, climbs out adjusts his tee shirt. "Not now darling. "I'll order later". The disappointed car hop slowly skates back to her station.

Don walks into Leon's phone booth, pulls the plastic door closed. He pulls a wrinkled paper out of his wallet. Don looks at the faded phone number. A nervous silence hovers. Don pulls a pocket knife out of his back jean pocket. Don carves (Don Miller April 1963) into the counter. Don pauses..... He pushes a silver dime into the black phone. Don places his index finger into the black rotary phone. The silence breaks as the phone retracts each of the 7 numbers dialed.

"Hello is Barb there"? "This is Barb - Who's this"? "It's the guy with the piss yellow car". Barb turns down her 45 rpm record player". "Ha ha - I didn't say that. The cowboy in the 57 Chevy said that. How are you Don? I guess you were in no hurry to call me". "Ah - I've been a little busy. Hey Barb do you still need that scratch fixed"? "Yes! Come over tomorrow around 3:30. You can meet my parents and kid sister. She gets home from High school around 4". "Ah - meet your parents and kid sister. The entire family"? "Yeah then you can stay for dinner". "Stay for dinner? I a ah". "Don you said you would fix my car. I won't take no for an answer". "But - parents and dinner"? "I live at 3800 Lake Shore Drive. Just past Saint Mary's high school. See you tomorrow, Bye". CLICK - "Barb..... Hello Barb".

Don pauses .... looks at (Don Miller April 1963). Grabs the door handle. Pulls open the squeaky door. A brisk April wind hits Don's sweaty forehead. He hops in his car. A smiling car hop skates up. "Hey doll get me a coke in one of those root beer frosty mugs". "Sure thing Hun". Don checks out the trim car hop as she skates away. He pulls a cigarette out of his rolled up shirt sleeve, lights up takes a long drag, relaxes......

"A car filled with giggling girls, parks next to Don's car. "Hey are you Don Miller"? Don looks in the mirror, combs his hair. "That's what they call me". "Do you remember us"? "Not really - with all the girls in town chasing me. "I can't remember every gal that wants a ride in my yellow bomb". "I bet you remember my kid sister". Don drops his comb. "Kid sister"? "Yeah Sheryl see". Sheryl opens her door. She wears a gear shift knob around her neck. "Hi Don - I want to ride with you tonight". Don looks. "Oh shit - sorry I have to go". He jams his shift in-to reverse, pops his clutch, burns rubber, does a wheelie speeding west on 27th street.

CHAPTER 5 - EDDIE MEETS CANDI

THE NEXT DAY
Bell Rings - It's 3pm school's out. Eddie Harper grips school books jogs home. He glances across Pryor street. Eddie stares at a slim blonde with full bangs. She wears a flowered dress with a white sweater. She chews gum swings her purse, she struts along Pryor street. Eddie's mouth drops. "Holy shit, what a babe, What a bitchen hot babe". In the distance near the alley. She sees. Three tuff looking guys late teens, smoking sporting sunglasses. Their hair is greased. They wear jeans, T-shirts, the back of their tarnished leather jackets reads - Ferraro Brothers.

The blonde grabs her purse with both hands. Joe Ferraro lowers his sun glasses. "Hey fine hen. What's happening"? She ignores them, speeds up. Vinnie Ferraro says. "Not so fast bitch, we're talking to you. Let's have some fun". Vinnie pulls her white sweater. Joe pulls at her purse. She hangs on with both hands. Dave Ferraro pulls the blonde's arms back behind her. "Joe what's in that freaking purse"? Vinnie rips her dress. She screams. "No no help. Somebody help me". Vinnie covers her mouth. "Shut up bitch. I hear you gave it to the whole football team. Now you give it to us".

Eddie looks, drops his books, flies across the street. Eddie lowers his shoulder crashes into Vinnie's back. Vinnie flies into the gutter. Joe and Dave drop the purse. Dave swings at Eddie. Eddie blocks, punches Dave. Dave hits the concrete. Joe tackles Eddie. Eddie looks up, Blondie picks up her purse. "Run girl run". She stares at Eddie. Joe and Eddie roll around, Eddie punches Joe. Blondie kicks Joe. Dave grabs Blondie, she knees him in the balls. Dave grabs his crotch screams, hits the sidewalk. Vinnie gets up, pulls a switch blade. "Say hello to my little friend". Vinnie stabs at Eddie. Eddie blocks - knocks the blade to the ground.

Don Miller cruising Pryor Street, sees Eddie. Don jumps out of his yellow coupe. Don decks Vinnie. Eddie Decks Dave. Joe Ferraro gets up. He staggers, screams. "That's Don Miller - Let's get the flock out of here". The three Ferraro brothers, limp, stumble down the alley.

Blondie pulls on her sweater, adjusts her ripped dress, brushes her hair. She stares into Eddie's eyes. "My name is Candi. Are you Popeye". Eddie smiles. "Hi, I'm Eddie Harper. But the girls in this town call me Eddie. This is my friend Don". Candi smiles. "Wow my lucky day. I meet Popeye and Superman. Somebody pinch me, I must be dreaming".

Don smirks, makes eye contact with Eddie. Blood drips onto Pryor street. "Harper I have clean rags in my car. Let's go, I'll give you guys a ride home". They walk to Don's car. Eddie picks up his books. Candi struts, twirls her blonde hair.

Don drives. Candi sits on Eddie's lap, she wraps his bloody hand. "Don thanks - But I had those guys. Did you see that bloody nose I gave Joe? And Candi here nailed Dave right in the nuts". Eddie laughs - "Dave was on rubber leg street. "Hell yeah - what a freaking rumble". Don downshifts. "Harper I know you could take those greasers. Friends help friends, people help people, remember Al's speech". They laugh.

Candi looks. "Hey Don patch out". Don looks. "What"? "Patch out, I just love it when guys lay rubber". Don looks at Eddie. Eddie shrugs his shoulders. "Ah what the hell - do it Don. Give the lady a show". "Ah okay - I hope officer Goldstein is at the donut shop". Don revs his engine, pops the clutch. squealing tires, a cloud of smoke rises. Don's tires burn rubber onto the quiet neighborhood street. Candi screams. "That was so cool. I love it when guys patch out".

Eddie winks at Don. "Candi what school do you go to"? "Harper - Harper Valley High, and you"? "Bay View senior class". Eddie looks. "Candi did anyone ever tell you - that you look like Jane Mansfield". John reacts! holds a laugh. Candi looks in the side mirror. "Ha you're funny. One time this toad guy said I looked like Sandra Dee". Don spins his head, looks at Candi. (Mumbles) "Terry the toad, that rascal".

Candi turns Don's rear view mirror. Pulls her blonde bangs, applies more red lipstick. "Hey Don, I bet you can get us some hard stuff. I bet ya, I bet ya, I bet you can". Don shakes his head. Pulls his rear view mirror. "Not today girl. I'm on my way to a job. I'm running late. Where do you live"? Candi pouts, crosses her arms. "3-8-0-0 Lake shore drive". Don looks! "What - where"? "3800 Lake shore drive". Don serves into oncoming traffic, tires screech beep beep. Candi crashes into Don. He serves back, Candi collides with Eddie. "Don my man, woo cat easy, trying to get us killed". Don downshifts, recovers, slows the yellow coupe to a crawl.

"Candi you, you live at 3800 Lake shore drive"? "Yep sure do. What's wrong is that to far. Don't you have enough gas"? Don lights a cigarette. "You live right by Saint Mary's High school"? "Yep - I would never go to that school. Those girls have to wear, blue and white uniforms, yuck. And there's no boys there - Boring". Don inhales a long drag. "I was on my way there, before I ran into your little rumble. Do you know Barb"? Candi swallows her gum. "My older sister, you know her. What's up"? Don tosses his cigarette. "Barb wants me to fix a scratch on her Corvette".

Candi flips her blonde hair. "Oh so you're the guy, Barb talks about". Eddie punches Don's shoulder. "Don you son of a bitch. You finally called the blonde bombshell. Hell yeah"! Candi elbows Eddie. "Who you calling bombshell. That's my sister, and she's way way to old for you Eddie". "Lay off girl it's just guy talk. Anyway Barb knows me too". Candi crosses her arms. "Yeah she does. How's that"? Eddie winks at Don. "I put ethel in her car many of times". Don, Eddie laugh, slap five. Candi looks.

Don shifts gears speeds up, looks at Candi. "So white corvette Barb is your sister, and your father is Ben Midway owner of Jiffy Trucking". "You got that right. What's the big freaking deal"? Don, Eddie make eye contact. Eddie flips out. "What a small world. That's crazy". "Hang on Harper it gets crazier". Eddie looks. "How's that"? Don changes lanes - shifts, passes cars. "After I fix Barb's car, she wants me to meet her parents and stay for dinner. So Harper I guess you're invited too. Sorry bud we are almost there". Candi stares at Eddie. "Neat that sounds like a great idea". Eddie sits up, boasts. "No problem Don my man. I know how to handle parents. Smile, toss in a few compliments. Heck it's a freaking breeze". Candi points. "Don turn, Lake Shore Drive".

Don downshifts, the yellow coupe purrs, hugs the road as it turns right. The 1932 ford crawls up a long drive, lined with large oak trees, towards a massive brick home resting on top of a hill. The boys eyes open wide as a large lake sparkles in the distance. Candi casually files her nails. She looks up - points. "There's Barb. She did her hair on a week night? Hmm wonder why".

Barb poses next to her glowing white corvette. Her blonde hair - styled up with large curls. She wears tight black Capri pants. Black stiletto heels strapped around her ankles. A white top, lipstick, eye shadow, false eyelashes and jewelry. Barb jumps waves. "Hi Don you made it". Barb looks. Her mouth drops. "Candi why are you crushing with Don Miller and Ed.... Eddie Harper"? "Lay off Barb. "Popeye here, I mean Eddie saved me from the Ferraro brothers. Then Don came along, just like the Superman". Candi jumps out. She hugs the boys as they exit Don's car. Candi holds up Eddie's bloody hand. "See" Barb looks. "Eddie what happened"? "This - oh it's nothing! A punk pulled a blade.... I punched it out of his hand.... No problem". Candi hugs Eddie. "My hero. Come on guys let's go inside".

Candi hangs onto Eddie as they walk two flights of stairs. Barb opens the door of the large brick home. A man about 40 wears a suit and sports a flat top haircut. He watches the news as he reads the newspaper. A woman wearing a long dress, heels, styled hair, ties her apron as she sets the large mahogany dinner table. This is Ben and Judy Midway. Candi yells across the large living room. "Mom dad I'm home. I brought a few friends with me. "This is Eddie and Don". Ben and Judy smile. Ben gets up, walks over to greet the boys. Judy unties her apron. They shake the boy's hands.

Judy looks. "Eddie what happened"? Eddie plays it up... Looks around. "Ah - Oh this, it's nothing Mrs. Midway". Candi boasts. "Eddie's my hero. He saved me". Ben looks down through his reading glasses. "Candace what happened"?

"On my way home, the Ferraro gang tried to take my purse. And do other stuff like cop a feel under my dress. See it's ripped". Judy looks at Ben. "Eddie heard me scream. He ran to save me, just like Popeye does". Eddie brags. "Ah it was nothing Mr. and Mrs. Midway". Barb looks. Candi turns up her volume. "First they pulled at my purse. Then they pulled at my top. Then I screamed. So a guy covered my mouth. Then another guy held my arms". Ben's face turns flush. "Then Vinnie pulled a 6 inch switch blade. I was so scared". Judy hugs Candi. Candi looks at Eddie. "Then Eddie came running. He punched that switch blade out of Vinnie's hand. They let go of me. Then Don appeared, just like Superman. When the Ferraro gang saw him. They ran down the alley. It was so cool".

Ben hugs Candi. He shakes the boys hands, using both hands, again and again. Judy sits pours a drink. Ben releases the hand shake. He pulls his handkerchief, wipes his forehead. "I've told officer Goldstein about those hoods on Pryor street. Thank you so much for saving our little Candi". Candi pouts. "Dad I'm 17". Ben hugs Candi. Waves his finger. "I've told you princess time and time again. No short cuts. Stay off Pryor street. Judy take a look at Eddie's hand. Let me know if Doctor Ben Casey should stop by". "Yes dear". Judy hands her drink to Ben. She walks Eddie towards the kitchen. Candi follows.

Ben grabs Don's shoulder. "Thanks again Don. Barbara tells me you are going to fix that big scratch on the corvette's hood". Ben winks. "Oh yes sir, I brought all my tools". Barb grabs her purse. "Great let's fix it before dinner". Barb pulls Don out the front door. Ben smiles.

CHAPTER 6 - BEN MIDWAY PROMISES A FAVOR

Judy Midway yells. "Dinner's ready". The aroma of grilled stake fills the large dining room. Eddie and Don sit at a neatly set large mahogany table. Burning candles reflect off the china plates. Don runs his hand across the smooth glass finish of the mahogany. Ben hands Don a platter of sizzling T- bone steaks. "Don, Barbara tells me you're a wiz at motor engines. I'm always looking for good mechanics at Jiffy Trucking. Want a job? It pays very well". Don flops a juicy steak onto his plate. "Ah no thanks Mr. Midway. Right now I like to work on my own". "I understand Don". Ben pauses, rests his fine silverware on his cloth napkin. He rests his elbows on the table. "Boys if you ever need anything, anything at all. No matter how big or small. Please let me know, understand"! "Yes sir".

Judy pours coffee. "Eddie, Barb told me you work at Al's service station". Ben looks reacts. "Al Dawson! Eddie you work for Al"? "Yes sir - Mr. Midway do you know Al"? A warm glow shines on Ben's face. "I sure do. We served in Korea together. I remember it like yesterday, Pork Chop Hill. Al was only 19. We were ambushed, out gunned, out numbered . Al Dawson took charge. Wow! I'll never forget how fast he moved and fired two machine guns one in each hand". Ben bows his head. "He saved many men that day. Al Dawson's a true war hero". Eddie nods. "Yes sir - Al's in the reserves. If we go to war, those Russians are in for it". Judy sips her coffee. "I don't think the Russians want to go to war, with our President Kennedy".

Candi looks down, pushes her peas around her plate. "Mom I don't want to go to Harper Valley's senior prom this year". Judy places her cup on it's saucer. "Why not dear? It's your last year. Every girl should experience the prom". "I want to go to the prom. But I want to go to Bay View's prom". Candi stares at Eddie. Eddie looks at Don. Ben adjusts his glasses. "Why's that. I paid a lot of money to send you to Harper Valley High". "Because dad, I heard that Bay View is having a new rock and roll band at their prom". Don Miller swallows his steak wipes his mouth. "Who's that - Pat Boone". Eddie laughs, chokes, spits his food into the fancy napkin. Don laughs, they slap five. The Midway's stare. The boys look, realize where they are. The laughter slows. They regain control, slowly slide into their seats.

Candi points her fork at Don. "No stupid - The Beat Boys". Don grabs a napkin, wipes his tears of joy. "Never heard of them". Candi twirls her fork. "To bad for you. They are a far out rock and roll band from California". Don drops his napkin. "Rock and roll band? Candi get real. First the plane crash, we lost two great guitarist, Buddy Holly, Ritchie Valens. The day February 3rd 1959". John points at his chest. "My license plate, in case you haven't noticed. Then 3 years ago Elvis stopped playing his guitar". Don looks down shakes his head. "Rock and roll has never been the same".

Candi looks at Eddie. "I want to see the Beat Boys at Bay View's prom, if someone asks me". Eddie points to his plate. "Mrs. Midway this meal is outstanding. Were you trained as a professional chef? Do you know Julia Child"? Judy Midway smiles touches her hair. "Thank you Eddie. I learned helping my mother cook after school".

Ben sips coffee. "Don I have two front row tickets, for the stock car races down at Elm Grove. I promised to take Barbara, I can't make it. Can you take her Friday"? Barb's face flushes. "Dad" Don swallows. "Front row sir, thee front row, Wow! Sure I'll go". Ben smiles. "Okay it's a date then Friday night". Barb covers her face. "I'm so embarrassed". Judy stands. "Come on girls help me with the cake". They walk into the kitchen.

Ben pours a drink. "I can't thank you boys enough for saving Candi from those hoods. I should give Al Dawson a call. The two of us can take care of that Ferraro gang. Ben pounds his mahogany table. Just like the old days, Dawson and I would take on anyone". Ben lights a his pipe. "Eddie tell Al, Semper Fi (Save the red Eagle)". Eddie looks at Don. "Sure will Mr. Midway. By the way sir, what does (Save the red Eagle) mean"? Don stops. Ben rolls his pipe. "That's a secret, I pray you boys and my daughters never experience".

Judy and daughters enter. They serve cake with ice cream. After desert Ben walks the boys to the door. Barb and Candi help Judy clear the table. Ben grabs Eddie's shoulder. Looks into his eyes. If you guys ever need anything, anytime ask me, I Owe you"! "Sure will. Goodbye Mr. Midway Mrs. Midway". They shake hands, hug the girls. Walk out the large front door.

Barb holds her head. "Dad I feel so stupid - mom". "What's wrong dear"? Barb flips her long blonde hair. "Girls don't ask guys out. Guys ask". Ben picks up his newspaper. "So - I'm a guy, and I asked". Laughter fills the large room. Judy hugs Barb. "Dear you're 21 you better find a husband soon. Do you want to be an old maid"? "Oh mom you're so old fashion". Barb and Candi walk up the stairs. Candi stops. "Do you think Eddie Harper will ask me to prom"? "Don't know sis, he seems so immature".

Ben hands the phone to Judy. "Call your friend at the Mayor's office. I hope she's working late". "Why Ben, is something wrong"? "Yes hurry - I need two front row tickets for the races this weekend". "Oh - Ben". Judy dials the heavy black phone. Ben smiles puffs his pipe.

CHAPTER 7 - MEET JERRY HARPER

Chip walks out his front door. It's a busy Saturday afternoon in the neighborhood. He waves to Mrs. Johnson pulling weeds from her fine manicured green lawn. Around the corner grandpa Bud puffs his pipe, waves walks his poodle dog. Down the street children run play kick the can. In the alley off Delaware avenue a pick up game of baseball plays on. Crash! Another window shattered, kids run.

In the distance Chip walks to a modest single story home. Chip knocks. A man about 40 years in a wheelchair opens the door. He smiles. "Chip, what a surprise come in". He wears a world war II veteran ball cap. This is Jerry Harper, Eddie's father. Chip walks into a clean modest home. A woman about 40, hair styled wearing a dress and apron irons cloths. She smiles. "Hello Chip. "How are you're mother and father"? "Their fine Mrs. Harper. Ah - Is Eddie home"? Mr. Harper rolls his wheelchair. "Eddie is upstairs doing homework. Can we help you son"? Chip removes his ball cap. Pushes his hair to the side. "I - ah came to ask Eddie a favor, kind of". "Is something wrong son"? Chip bends his cap. "Ah not really, well maybe sort of".

Viola Harper stops ironing. "Chip do you want me to call your mother"? Tears come to Chip's eyes. "No! Mrs. Harper, I don't want my family to think I'm a chicken". Jerry rolls his wheelchair. "Viola have Eddie meet Chip and I in the den". Jerry winks. Bring us your homemade cookies too". "Yes dear". Jerry wheels his chair towards the den. Chips follows, walks into the den.

Chip looks! Posters of world war II, President Eisenhower and Kennedy cover all four walls. A large American flag hangs over Jerry's desk. Eddie walks in. "Chip? What's up, where's Wally"? "Son, Chip came by to ask you a favor". Eddie crosses his arms. "No you can't borrow my catchers mitt. Is that it, I'm sort of busy with my studies". Chip hangs his head, tears build. Jerry stares at Eddie, pounds his desk. "Edward (shape up get serious)". Eddie tones down. "Yes sir".

Chip wipes his tears. "There's this bunch of guys. The big one is in the 8th grade. His name is Butch". Eddie places his hands on his hips. "Yeah Butch Davis, I know his older brother Randy. What about"? Jerry wheels holds Chip's arm. "Relax Chip you're among friends". "Butch takes my lunch money. He pushes me down". Chip's voice cracks, tears build. "He says he's going to knock my teeth out". Chip cries. Jerry looks at Eddie. Viola Harper yells. "Jerry is everything okay"? "Everything is fine dear". Jerry wheels closes the door.

"Son do your parents know about this"? Chip quickly shakes his head. "Oh no sir, I don't want them to think I'm a sissy or chicken to fight. I would but". Chip extends both arms. "But Butch is real big". Jerry squeezes Chip's arm.

"Don't be ashamed Chip. Courage works in strange ways. Back in 1944 the battle of the bulge. I was 20 and scared silly". Tears form in Eddie's eyes. He grabs his dad's shoulder. Jerry adjusts his cap. "A grenade rolled to Rocky my sergeant. Chip a mighty courage came into me. I jumped and covered that bomb. I saved Rocky's life, but in the process I lost my legs. I've been in this chair for almost 20 years. Not a day goes by that I regret this chair. I'm honored I had the opportunity to serve my country". Jerry and Eddie look at the large flag.

"Mr. Harper is sergeant Rocky still in the army"? "We lost touch". Jerry smiles. "Last I heard Rocky started a (motorcycle club) in California". Jerry looks at his world war II posters. Viola enters, carrying a tray of milk and cookies. Chip smiles. "Oh boy thank you Mrs. Harper". "You're welcome, say hi to your mom". She exits. Jerry wheels close to Chip. "When you need it courage appears. Look Butch in the eyes. He will back off". Chip bites a cookie. "Really sir, that would be great". "You get home now son. Tell your dad I said Semper Fi (Save the red Eagle)". "Yes sir I will. Bye Mr. Harper, bye Eddie". Chip skips out the room.

Jerry closes the door, stares at Eddie. "Edward take care of this Butch character. Our secret, no one knows about this, understand". Eddie pushes up his sleeves. "Yes sir our secret. I'll take care of Butch".

29

CHAPTER 8 - EDDIE MEETS MARTY JENSEN

MONDAY MORNING - APRIL 25, 1963

Jane Crawford neatly dressed opens her front door. Wally, Chip carry books walk to school. "Have a nice day boys. Wally isn't Eddie walking with you to school"? "Heck no mom, Eddie told me he had early track practice".

Eddie jogs towards school. With Bay View high school in sight, Eddie makes a right hand turn, jogs toward Trowbridge grade school. Up the block he sees Butch holding the arms of a crying young boy, as his two cronies empty the pockets of the terrified boy. Eddie runs, grabs Butches neck from behind, pushes the cronies. "Give the boy his money back, or I'll punch Butch in the nose". Butch twists, waves his arms. "Don't give it back, he's nothing. His dad's a cripple. The three of us can kick his ass". The two cronies drop the lunch money. "No Butch he's in high school. We ain't messing with no teenager. Let's go". The cronies run. Eddie tightens his grip. "Ouch, let me go I didn't do anything". Eddie looks, the small boy sobs, picks up his lunch money. "Small fry you okay? What's your name". "Marty - Marty Jensen, what's yours"? "I'm Eddie - Eddie Harper". Marty smiles. Thanks a lot Eddie I'm okay". Eddie tightens his grip. "OUCH" "Marty don't worry about this fat punk. He will never mess with you again". "Gee thanks" - Marty skips towards school.

Eddie tightens his grip. "Ouch - Let me go or I'll tell my big brother". "Ha your brother Randy doesn't faze me Butch". Eddie holds Butches right arm behind his back as he pushes him up the street. A Baby Ruth candy bar hits the ground. "Wait that's mine". Eddie grabs it, pockets it. "Who did you steal this from"? Eddie grips. "Ouch, where are we going"? "Have a talk with your mom". "Ah - my moms not home". "Yeah right, on a school day. I'm sure your moms home".

They approach a large brick two story home. A pink Cadillac glows in the horseshoe drive. "Listen up fats. Eddie twists Butches arm. If you ever bully Chip Crawford, little Marty Jensen, anyone. You get a bloody nose, you got that punk"! "Okay okay" tears form in Butch's eyes. "I got it. Just don't hit me". He let's go of Butch. Eddie tucks in his shirt, combs his hair, rings the doorbell.

A lady mid 30's, sporting a fancy dress, hairstyle and jewelry opens the door. The aroma of perfume fills the air. "Butchy what's wrong"? "Hello Mrs. Davis, please allow me to introduce myself. I'm Eddie Harper a senior at Bay view High school. There seems to be a problem with young Butch here". She lights a long cigarette.

"Problem, what problem"? "Well Mrs. Davis, this past school year, young Butch has bullied Chip Crawford and other young lads for their milk and lunch money". Eddie jesters. "The poor lads have to attend class and study in a hungry state of mind. Judging by Butches physique here". Eddie sizes vertical and horizontal boxes around Butch. "He uses the extra coin for candy bars and ice cream". Eddie pulls the Baby Ruth bar, waves it at Mrs., Davis. She puffs her long cigarette. "Butchy is this true"? Tears run down his face. "Yes momma". She frowns. "Wait till your father gets home! Go to your room". Butch cries, runs into the large home.

"Thank you for bring this to my attention. I'll call Jane Crawford apologize and repay her". Eddie waves his arms. "Oh no Mrs. Davis we can't do that". "Do what"? Eddie points to himself. "Chip came to me. Not to his big brother. Not to his parents. You see Mrs. Davis, Chip doesn't want his family to know he's been bullied". Eddie jesters. "It's a guy thing". She twists her diamond necklace. "I see, so how do I repay the Crawford's"?

Eddie paces rubs his chin. Points his index finger to the blue sky.. "Let's see hear, fifty cents a week since September. Today is April 25th, 8 x 5 carry the one, minus Christmas vacation". Eddie shadow draws. "A few sick days". Ah - Lets just round it off to $18.36". "Okay, how do I repay the Crawford's"? "Pay me. I'll get the money back to the Crawford's.

Mrs. Davis opens her fancy purse, looks for cash. "$18.36 can I write you a check"? "Sure I work at Al's he'll cash it". Then I'll slip the cash into the Crawford's cookie jar". Eddie Jesters. "No problem Mrs. Davis. It's not a problem at all. Write that check".

Mrs. Davis stops, looks at Eddie. "You work for Al - Thee Al Dawson"? "Yes ma'am - Bring that pink Cadillac in. That left tire looks low". Mrs. Davis touches her perfectly styled hair. "How's Al? Is he still a bachelor"? "He sure is. Al says as long as he's in the reserves, he stays single. Just in case we go to war". Mrs. Davis flicks her cigarette. Her high heels rub it into the concrete. She smirks. "War! no way. Not with President Kennedy. The Russians are afraid of him". She pulls a fountain pen. "Today is April 25, 1963. Spell your name". "E-D-D-I-E H-A-R-P-E-R" The fountain pen glides. "Eighteen dollars and thirty six cents" She hands the check to Eddie. He looks.

"Mrs. Davis your penmanship is outstanding". She smiles. Eddie stuffs the check in his shirt, shakes her hand. "It's been an honor meeting you, and please tell Councilman Mr. Davis he's doing a fantastic job". She smiles. Eddie turns, struts down the long driveway. Mrs. Davis waves. "Oh Eddie tell Al". She pauses. "Please tell Al Dawson I said hello". "I sure will ma'am". She looks down, twists her diamond necklace, walks into her massive home.

Eight hours later a black clear coat Cadillac parks next to the pink Cadillac. A man mid 30's wearing a business suit exits. Carrying a brief case in his left hand. He opens his mail box. Walks into his large home.

Mrs. Davis fills water glasses on the dinner table. She smiles. "Welcome home Hank". He smiles. "Hello Crystal". Hank kisses Crystal. "How were things at city hall dear"? Hank loosens his tie. "Tense with the election coming up. Everyone is stressed out". Hank shifts through the mail. "Anything exciting happen today? Any gossip at the beauty parlor"? Crystal looks at her nails. "I had to cancel my appointment. Butch was home". Hank looks up adjusts his glasses. "Is he sick, measles chicken pox"? Crystal touches Hank's shoulder. "Butch is fine dear.

This morning a very clean cut young man escorted him home. It appears Butch has been bullying kids on there way to school. He takes their lunch or milk money". Hank backs away, looks upstairs. "Takes milk money? We give Butch plenty of money"? Crystal walks to the bar. "Butch admitted it. Heck he's bullied and taken this year, almost twenty dollars from the Crawford boy". Hank throws down the mail. "Wayne Crawford's boy. He runs the VFW post. Hell if this gets out, we can kiss my re-election bye bye".

Crystal hands Hank a drink. "Don't worry dear, I took care of it". Hank chugs his drink. Removes his belt. "I'm going to teach that boy a lesson". "Oh dear don't be to ruff on him". Hank jogs up the stairs, down the long hall. Belt in hand opens a bedroom door.

Baseball posters of the Milwaukee Braves and Hank Aaron cover the walls. Bats, balls, baseball gloves clutter the large two bed room. Butch reading a comic book, looks. "Dad no wait not the belt, I didn't do anything". "Taking lunch money, bend over". "No dad wait, I won't do it anymore". Hank slaps Butches butt. Butch screams, tears run down his chubby cheeks. "Waa Waa - I'm sorry". Hank stops. Butch pulls up his pants, crawls onto his bed. Buries his head in his pillow crying. "I'm taking the money out of your allowance, understand young man". "Yes sir".

A seventeen year old boy holding school books walks in. Hank buckles his belt, adjusts his glasses. "Randy, Butch is grounded. He will not be attending the Braves game with us next month". Randy drops his books on his desk. "But dad, the LA Dodgers will be in town". Randy picks up a baseball. "Butch waited a long time to see Sandy Koufax, get his autograph". Butch pounds his bed. "Waa Waa". "Son you boys must learn. If you misbehave then there are consequences later in life. Your mother has dinner ready. Wash up I'll see you at the table". "Yes sir". Hank walks out.

Randy sits on Butches bed. Tears are in his eyes, he turns to Randy. "That stupid Eddie Harper he thinks he's all it". Butch throws his tear soaked pillow across the room. "Why did you get the belt"? "Eddie's a squealer. I was just having fun with a small fry. Harper shows up acts like superman. Stops the fun, takes me home, tells mom. Now I can't go to the Braves game". Butch cries, punches his bed. Randy picks up a bat. "Harper what a freaking tattletale squealer, that's lame. I never liked him or his click. They walk around school wearing their letter sweaters, like they own the joint". Butch grabs Randy's bat. "I want you to beat up Eddie for me". Randy looks! "I can't mess with him little brother. Eddie's on the varsity wrestling team". Butch swings his bat. "Damn who can we get to beat up Eddie"? "That's a tuff task Butch. Harper has lots of friends. He's very popular. Let me think about this". Randy grabs the bat. Rests it on his shoulder, paces the room.

Randy looks at a red peddle driven fire engine, in the corner of their large bedroom. He swings his bat. "Wait a minute Butch I have a better idea". Butch stands, shadow boxes. "What - what is it"?

"Eddie brags about Don Miller chauffeuring him and his buddies to the senior prom". "Chauffeuring! What's that"? "Don Miller drives them to the prom". Butch Laughs. "I'm sure, how can they all fit in his tiny car"? "Miller has tons of cars stupid". Randy swings his bat. "Wow I got it". Randy sits on the bed. Butch shadow boxes. "What bro what"? "You know that old a banded car by the fire station". "Yeah the beat up black one, with the broken window". "Well Butch last week, old fireman Gus got it running". "So who cares"? "Butch do you know Otis"? "The drunk guy yeah so". "Here's my plan, to get back at Harper and all his jock stuck up friends". Butch shadow boxes. "What is it"?

Randy paces the entire large room. "I know where Gus keeps the keys for that old bomb. We will visit Gus, let him talk about his old army days. When Gus goes to the can, I'll nab the keys". Butch stops. "Are we going to steal the car"? "Not really, it will look like Otis took the car". "Otis! He can't drive". "That's right little brother. "Listen up. I'll take two liquor bottles out of dad's cabinet". Butch slaps his forehead. "Two bottles, why"? "Quiet listen up. During lunch I overheard that dork Wally Crawford. The jocks are going to meet at his house before prom. When Miller picks them up, I figure he will drive KK avenue all the way to the Bay View High school gym". Butch hands on hips. "How do you know that"? "Miller always cruises KK avenue". "Why"? "He likes the new pavement, and he brags on how he hits all the green lights". "Who cares! "What about Otis"?

Randy points. "There is one four way stop on KK avenue". Butch jumps. "So - what about beating up Eddie"? Randy holds his hand up. "Otis sits in the junk car at the four way stop. I'll tell Otis, when I wave if you can cross KK in five seconds. You win another bottle of whiskey".

Crystal Davis yells. "Boys time for dinner". "Coming mother". Randy continues. "When we see Miller's car leave his stop sign, I'll wave to drunk Otis. Crash - that heavy old boat will cream and plow over Miller's car". Butch jumps. "Wow cool plan". Randy looks in the mirror. Pushes his hair. "Yeah - Don Miller's car gets demolished. Eddie and his stuck up jock friends will be in no condition to dance at their senior prom, to bad". Butch shadow boxes. "Cool plan Randy. I hope Eddie gets real bloody". Randy slaps five.

"As for Otis, he might spend time in jail. But hey what the hell, he likes it there anyway". Hank Davis yells. "Boys did you hear your mother? Dinners ready now". "Coming father". The boys smile run out the room..

35

CHAPTER 9 - RIDE TO PROM

LATE AFTERNOON - MAY 1963
A fresh red painted 1958 Chevy Impala glows in the afternoon sun. The large whitewalls twirl as it slowly parks on the Crawford's concrete driveway. Don Miller combs his hair. He exits the American made car, slowly closes his drivers side door. Don pulls a rag out of his back pocket of his blue jeans. He wipes a finger print from the side door. Don looks, wipes the hood of the red car. He adjusts his pack of smokes into the sleeve of his white tee shirt as he walks to the front door, rings the door bell.

Wayne Crawford opens the door. Standing behind Wayne are Walley, Eddie and Clarence dressed in black suits, white shirts black ties. Jane Crawford and Chip play cards. Wayne smiles. "Don come in". Wayne looks. "Don is that a new car"? "No sir, she's 5 years old. I just put a fresh coat of paint on her. Wally and the gang look sharp. So I wanted their ride to the big dance to look sharp".

Wally chugs his soda. "Let's go guys, Eddie wants to stop at Al's first". "Wally what's the hurry"? "Mom I want to get there before our dates arrive". Jane looks. "In my day the boy would meet the girl's parents. Then escort her to the dance". Eddie combs his hair. "Mrs. Crawford, Don has this superstitious thing. When he paints a car the break in ride is just guys. No girls allowed. We'll catch our dates at the dance no problem". Wayne smiles. "Jane it's the new generation. Everyone has to do their own thing". They chuckle. Jane looks. "Well you boys be careful". Wayne opens the front door. "Have fun boys. Wally we'll leave the light on for you". Eddie picks up a large marble bag. "Let's go gents, we have places to go and people to meet". Chip winks at Eddie.

Eddie swings his marble bag as the four boys walk to Don's car. "I got dibs on the front seat. You two jokers can have the back". Don Looks. "Careful guys the paint is fresh". The whitewalls twirl, shine. Don slowly backs out the driveway. "Harper what's up, aren't you a little old for marbles"? The gang laughs. Eddie smirks as he opens the bag. Ben Franklin silver half dollars and silver quarters shimmer in the late afternoon sun. "What did you do man? Rob a bank". Eddie laughs. "Hell no, this is the paperboys coin. He has to pay his bill in paper. Al needs the change. It works out. Stop at Al's, I'll cash this coin in. Plus I have a $18.36 check to cash too. Hell I'm loaded".

Wally, Clarence lean forward. They study the glowing silver coins. Wally taps Eddie's back. "Where did you get the check"? Eddie ties the bag closed. He squirms, looks out his side window. "Ah, I ah cut a few lawns". Eddie twists, "Ouch what the hell is this"? Eddie holds up a seat belt. Don grabs it. "That's a seat belt Harper. Some day every car is going to have them". Wally, Clarence dig, grab their belts, stare. "Don what are they for"? "Safety - clamp them around you". Eddie grabs the belt out of Don's hand. "Not me boys, It will wrinkle my fresh dry cleaned pants". Don smiles.

"Harper I heard through the grapevine. In the future, everyone in the car has to wear one". "Ha not me, if I don't wear one Don, is the creature from the black lagoon going to get me". Clarence and Wally laugh. Don shakes his head. "Worse Eddie! In the future if you don't wear a seat belt, the cops will give you a ticket. It will be the law". Eddie shakes. "A law! Who told you that garbage? Where are we Russia? This is America. President Kennedy would never pass that law". Clarence interjects. "My daddy read that seat belts are a good idea. (Click) I'm wearing mine". Wally buckles his belt. "What the heck, I'll try mine too. Just like at Dandelion amusement park.

Eddie smirks shakes his head. "Not me gents. That belt will wrinkle my pants. The only thing that's going to wrinkle my pants tonight is my date. Hey hey". The car fills with laughter. Don downshifts slows down. "Yeah - you're right Harper. I've raced these streets for years, no accidents. These belts are for the birds". Don stops at the four way stop.

Don rips his seat belt, throws it out the passenger window. Barely missing Eddie's face. Don and Eddie laugh slap five. Don crawls through the intersection laughing, looking to his right as they watch the seat belt tumble down the road.

From his back seat Wally sees a black car to his left speeding through the stop sign. "Stop stop - Don stop"! (Screech Bang) The black car plows into Don's door. Don's car rolls, Eddie and Don fly out. Don's head crashes onto the cement pavement. Eddie and Don lay unconscious. Don's red car rests upside down. Wally, Clarence knocked out, remain in the car.

Otis the driver of the black car, stumbles out holding a bottle of whiskey. Randy and Butch Davis run to the bleeding mangled bodies of Eddie and Don Miller. Randy yells. "Hey Otis, look what you did". Otis bottle in hand staggers down Ellen avenue. Randy and Butch laugh slap five. "Look Butch laying in the street gutters. The two Bay View tuff guys. They don't look so tuff now. Oh Donnie, what happened to your new red car? Not even the great Don Miller will be able to fix that wreck. It's time for the junk yard Miller".

Butch swift kicks Eddie in the ribs. "Hey Harper you going to run and tell my mom. You rat fink. Get up Mr. tuff guy". Butch spits on Eddie's bleeding face. Eddie's eyes crack half open. Randy kicks Eddie again and again into his broken ribs. "Harper pay back is a bitch isn't it. Don't mess with my little brother". Randy looks. A crowd begins to gather. Randy Davis kneels over Eddie. "Call an ambulance. They are my friends". A middle age woman says, "Oh my is that Don and Eddie Harper? What happened"? Randy Davis points. A drunk guy ran the stop. Hit and run". Butch shakes his head. "Yes that's what happened". In the overturned car, Wally and Clarence slowly wake up. Walley pushes Clarence. "You okay"? "Yeah ouch. You okay"? "I guess I'm okay. Look Don and Eddie".

Wally and Clarence unbuckle their seat belts. Crawl out of the upside down car. Randy and Butch Davis ease away from the scene. Clarence points. "Look Walley Don's head is split wide open blood everywhere". Walley kneels over Eddie holds his bloody head. "Hang in there, the ambulance is coming. We're going with you". Eddie coughs blood. "What the hell for? Are you guys doctors now? No go to our prom, we're seniors, it's our last one. Take care of Candi for me". Eddie grabs Wally's collar. Stares into his eyes. "I'll see you guys later. Don and I will be fine. Ain't that right Don"? He turns looks at Don. Eddie passes out.

The sounds of sirens grows louder. The onlookers cover their eyes, turn away cry. The flashing lights of the ambulance drives up. The paramedics see Don's bloody cracked skull. The driver shakes as they cover Don's face. Eddie and Don are lifted onto stretchers. They carry the boys into the ambulance. The siren blasts, the tires squeal, the ambulance drives away.

Two police officers arrive, They talk to Clarence and Wally. One officer finds the tied marble bag of silver coins. "Who does this money belong to"? Wally looks. "That's Eddie Harper's money officer". "Ernie file this under Eddie Harper property. Thank you boys. Good thing you were both wearing those new gadget seat belts. You're friends oh my". The officer writes. "Okay boys we have all the info for now. If we need anything we will call you". The police drive down KK avenue. The middle age woman asks. "Do you boys need a ride"? Clarence pouts. "No thanks ma'am.What a bummer, don't feel much like dancing know". Wally interjects. "Wait a minute Clarence. Why not go? They're in good hands. Eddie wants us to go. We have to tell the gang about Don and Eddie". "You bring up a good point Wally. Okay let's go, for Eddie and Don's sake". The woman points. "My cars over there follow me". Clarence and Wally hop into a Buick. The Buick drives KK avenue towards Bay View High school.

CHAPTER 10 - SAINT LUKES HOSPITAL ROOM - 222

Eddie wrapped in bandages hooked to machines lies unconscious. Two nurses tend to Eddie. Doctor Ben Casey walks in. Doctor Richard Kaye studies a chart. "What's the news Rick anything good"? Doctor Richard shakes his head. "Two young men hit by a drunk driver running a stop sign". Doctor Ben looks at the chart. "I hate days like this. How's Harper doing"? He took a massive blow to the head. Eddie's in a coma with multiple fractures. That had to be one Hell of an accident. Both sides of Eddie's ribs are shattered, busted up. He must have rolled and rolled". Doctor Ben reacts. "Damn drunk drivers". "Ben, Eddie's a fighter. I see that look in his eye. I believe he has a shot".

"Rick is Don Miller still in intensive care"? "No Ben". Ben hangs his head. "I know he took a massive blow. Don's skull was cracked wide open. He lost a large quantity of blood. (pause) Did Miller pass"? Eddie jerks! Doctor Rick tosses the chart. "I don't know Ben". "What! Don't know? Where's Don Miller"? "I wish I knew Ben. Here's all I know. A Leroy Johnson showed up. He walked into Don Miller's room. I heard some one whistling that famous Harlem Globe Trotters song, Ah - ahh (Sweet Georgia Brown). A minute or two later, I walked into the room. Bang go - The room was vacant, clean as a whistle, spic and span. As if - no one had used that room for a week".

A divine warm light enters room 222 (Glowing). The Crucifix on the wall slowly moves side to side. Eddie jerks. Nurses, doctors look. Their faces turn pale. "Rick is it still happy hour? I need a drink". "Me too Doctor Casey. Pinky's Bowling Alley next door, meet you there". The doctors break a slight smile, exit.

That evening in the school gym.

A sign reads - BAY VIEW'S SPRING PROM DANCE 1963.

Two hundred students and a few teachers fill the gymnasium. Girls are wearing formal dresses. Boys are dressed in suits and ties. Small clusters of girls chat. Groups of boys hang out, trying to act cool. On stage a band is setting up. Cookie, Terry, Sonny and Steve hang out at the punch bowl. Sonny looks around. "Anyone see Eddie, Clarence, or Wally, the bands about to start". Steve shakes his head. "No not a sign of all three". Terry sips his punch spiked with old harpers whiskey, adjusts his thick glasses. "Ha, Eddie's a no show unbelievable. He's bragged all year that, thee Don Miller was his personal chauffeur to senior prom. Eddie made sure every girl knew that".

Cookie combs his hair in the reflection of the punch bowl. "Hey Steve, I thought you graduated last year. What the hell you doing here"? Steve chugs his drink. "I did, I'm here with Laurie". Cookie pockets his greasy comb. "You still with that chick? Man she's yesterdays news. You let Curt run off to collage by himself. Just because of a stupid dame". Steve grabs Cookie's white shirt. "Calling me stupid, wanna step outside"? Terry and Sonny push, hold Steve and Cookie. "Steve easy does it". Steve raises both hands. "Okay okay I'm cool". Cookie looks in the punch bowl. "Toad you messed the hair. Heck I have better things on my mind, I'm out". Cookie reaches for his comb as he struts to a group of girls.

Sonny points. "On stage Principle Showers". An older man wearing a gray suit stands in front of a five man band. The band wears white pants with red and white stripped shirts. Principle Showers raises both hands. The crowd quiets. "Students welcome to Bay View high schools 1963 prom dance". The crowd roars. "Straight from California here are the Beat Boys". Females "scream". The lead singer grabs the mic. "A new song for all you pretty girls out there". The crowd "roars". The band jams. "Midwest girls are crisp. I really did the styles of their hair".

The dance floor fills. Terry twists bumps into Sonny. " Seen Eddie yet". "No man, to bad he's missing a hip band. (dancing) Hey look there's Wally and Clarence taking to Mary Rogers and that chick from Harper Valley High. Candi Midway she's crying". Sonny and Terry run off the crowed dance floor. Their dates continue dancing. Terry winded, adjusts his glasses. "Wally Clarence where's Eddie"? Wally grabs Terry. "Car accident, Eddie and Don are in the hospital". Candi "cries". Mary Rogers hugs Candi. Candi crying, "Oh my God, Eddie what hospital"? Clarence hands Candi a handkerchief. "Saint Luke's". "I'm leaving". Candi runs. Wally hugs his date. "Mary Ellen, Don and Eddie are in good hands. Let's keep it together we have to dance soon".

The song ends. The crowd "screams". Principle showers hops on stage. "Student our prom king and queen for 1963. Wally Crawford and Mary Ellen Rogers". The crowd "cheers". The beat boys sing. "It's your last year of school, be true to your girl or guy". Wally and Mary slow dance. "Wally I hope you change your mind". "About what"? "Are you still joining the army"? "For sure after a boss summer". Wally you're not scared"? "Scared - scared of what"? "A war what if we go to war"? Wally laughs. "No way anyone wants to mess with JFK".

CHAPTER 11 - THE COMA CONTINUES

LINCOLN MEMORIAL AUGUST 28, 1963

Martin Luther king Jr. civil rights activist and Baptist minister wears a suit as he speaks to 250,000 civil rights supporters. "I have a dream that one day this nation will rise up"………

Back at the Prom, the lighting is dim. The Beat Boys Play on. Dancing students along with Cookie, Wally, Mary Ellen, Clarence, Terry, Sonny, Steve and Laurie pack the dance floor.

SAINT LUKES HOSPITAL ROOM 222 - OCTOBER 1963

Eddie lies unconscious hooked to machines. Candi Midway sits near the window praying, reading the Bible . Doctor Richard Kaye holds a chart stands near Eddie. Doctor Ben Casey walks in. "How's he doing"? "No change Ben, Eddie's still in a semi coma. He has a strong will. I can see it in his eyes. Hell it's been four months". Doctor Richard throws his chart. Doctor Ben picks up the chart, turns pages. "We have to get Eddie out of that damn bed. His muscles will waste away". Candi stops reading. "I'm lost Ben any suggestions"? Ben looks at Eddie.

"I've read about patients half awake like Eddie. Rick say your head is under a shower and someone walks into the room. That's Eddie right now". Doctor Richard reacts! "Interesting concept Ben. Eddie knows people are in the room. He knows he's alive. But that's about it". Yes Rick, I've read about experiments performed at the Mayo Clinic". "Up in Rochester Minnesota"? "Yes, they put patients like Eddie on a tread mill. He wears a safety belt attached to the ceiling. Eddie will walk jog, its natural muscle memory for him. Rick starts writing. "I see hmm interesting". "Yes it is. This keeps the patients muscles strong and mind sharp".

Doctor Ben Casey looks at Candi. "Eddie wants to exercise. He's a fighter. Eddie wants to live". "The food Ben. Feed Eddie the best. Plenty of fruits and vegetables, fish, little sugar and no fried foods". Ben shakes his head. "I agree healthy food, exercise him twelve hours everyday. Hell when Eddie wakes up he will be like superman". Doctor Richard smiles. "Oh boy, Let's transfer Eddie as soon as possible. Cassius Clay and Sonny Liston watch out". The doctors laugh. Candi smiles wipes tears.

CHAPTER 12 - TIME MOVES ON

The Beat Boys play on. The dance floor is packed with happy dancing students. Steve and Laurie, Wally and Mary Ellen Rogers continue dancing. Principle Showers and the teachers watch.

DALLAS TEXAS - NOVEMBER 22, 1963 - 12:30 pm

The midnight blue convertible cruises Elm street through Dealey Plaza. President John F Kennedy waves to the happy cheering crowd, he stands and sits in the back seat of the convertible. BANG BANG - Shots fired. President Kennedy is hit. Jacqueline Kennedy age 34 holds JFK. The blue convertible speeds to Parkland Memorial hospital. President Kennedy is rushed to Trauma room #1. At 1pm that Friday afternoon President Kennedy age 46 is pronounced dead. America is shocked. The world mourns.

NOVEMBER 29, 1963 - WASHINTON DC

Three year old John Kennedy Jr. salutes his fathers casket.

BAY VIEW SCHOOL GYM - DIMLY LIT - DECEMBER 1963

The Beat Boys play to a full dance floor. Wally and Mary Ellen, Steve and Laurie slow dance.

MAYO CLINIC - FITNESS ROOM - FEBRUARY 9, 1964

Eddie eyes are half closed. He wears a shoulder harness that's tied to the ceiling. He stumbles and trips as he walks on a slow moving tread mill. A physical therapist watches closely. Two female nurses watch, sadly shake their heads, turn away. She points to a small black and white television. "Look Ed Sullivan". "Ladies and gentlemen the Beatles". A rock band of four young men. They wear black suits. ties, white shirts. They rock and shake their longer hair that is combed forward. Females in the audience scream and cry.

MAYO CLINIC - FITNESS ROOM - MARCH 7, 1965

Eddie stumbles and bumbles on his treadmill. The staff monitors him. A nurse looks at the black and white television. A newscaster wears a gray suit. His hair and mustache are gray. "Today President Johnson sent two battalions of marines to South Vietnam. That's the way it is today March 7, 1965.

CHAPTER 13 - AL DAWSON GOES TO VIETNAM

BAY VIEW SCHOOL GYM - DIMLY LIT - 1966

The Beat boys play to a packed dance floor. Wally and Mary Ellen dance. Wally combs his hair forward. Mary Ellen's style of dress has changed.

SOUTH VIETNAM JUNGLE - 1967

Two young American soldiers, Privates Sam Keller and Jim Dec are tied and beaten by nine Vietcong. An older American GI without a gun, hides in the brush. This is special forces green beret, Sergeant Al Dawson.

A Vietcong soldier drenches both GI's with gasoline. "I kill them now. I burn them to ashes". The young Americans break down cry. "No no please don't kill us. Help God help us". The eight other Vietcong laugh toast drink, sit to enjoy the burn to death torture. Sam Keller cries, screams. "Please please my wife just had a baby boy. God help us". Leroy Johnson appears, He stands next to Al Dawson.

The cocky Vietcong soldier lights a match. "I guess your God don't like you". The eight drunk Vietcong laugh. Leroy Johnson whistles (Sweet Georgia Brown). Al Dawson rises up, throws a large knife into the Vietcong's neck. Blood flies. Sam Keller screams. "Hey Jimmie Al Dawson's here".

Al Dawson dives over the brush. Grabs the dead man's gun. Al Dawson rolls, fires Bang Boom Bang Bang. Al kills the 8 drunk onlookers in seconds. Al unties the two young shook up rookie soldiers. "Sergeant first class Al Dawson here. Serial no. N3794N". "Al how did you find us"? "That's my job private Keller". "My wife just had a baby boy look". Sam Keller opens his wallet. Al Dawson holds a black and white photo. He sees a young woman wearing a bee-hive hair do. She is proud and smiling holding a baby boy.

Al smiles as he hands the photo back. "Congratulations private. That's a beautiful family you have. Take care of them. "You saved my life serge. I Owe you. What can I do for you? How can I repay you"? (Al stares into Sam's eyes). "Private that's life. We give a little take a little. In the end it evens out". Sam Keller shakes his head. "I'm not sure I understand serge". Al Dawson grabs Sam, they lock eyes. "Someday Sam I'll need help. Can I count on Sam Keller for help on that day"? Sam Keller smiles and salutes. "Yes sir I will never forget what you did for me and my family today". Al Dawson nods. "Okay troops move out".

CHAPTER 14 - TIC TOCK TIME MOVES ON

MAYO CLINIC - FITNESS ROOM - JULY 20, 1969

Eddie strapped into his harness, stumbles and trips on the slow moving treadmill. Doctors Ben Casey and Richard Kaye page through their clipboards. Two nurses watch Eddie. Doctor Ben shakes his head. "Rick it's been 6 years of exercise, 12 hours per day. Three square meals of fruit, vegetables and lean protein. There's little improvement. I can't explain this". "Yes Ben, it's sad. Eddie's family and friends have quit on him. No more visits. Many say pull the plug on Harper. I say no way. I refuse to. I see something in Eddie's eyes". "Yes Rick, I see it too".

In the corner of the fitness room a color television plays. A male newscaster says. "Apollo 11 has landed on the moon". Neil Armstrong says. "One small step for man. One giant leap for mankind". The newscaster signs off. "That's the way it is July 20, 1969.

BAY VIEW HIGH SCHOOL GYM - DIMLY LIT - 1970

The Beat Boys play on stage. The bands style of dress has changed. The Beat Boys wear longer hair. Students fill the dimly lit dance floor. Their style and way of dance has changed. Wally Crawford and Mary Ellen have aged seven years.

KENT STATE UNIVERSITY - MAY 4, 1970

Student march protesting the Vietnam war. The Ohio state National Guard watch. Male students burn their draft cards. BANG BANG - Shots are fired into the crowd of demonstrators, killing four and wounding nine. A screaming crying female arms raised, kneels over a dead male student.

MAYO CLINIC - FITNESS ROOM - NOVEMBER 4, 1979

Eddie stumbles and falls on his treadmill. Doctors Ben Casey and nurses monitor him. Ben Casey throws his clipboard. "Poor guy not one damn visitor in 10 years. They have given up. Not me - I feel something. I see something in Eddie's eyes. Everyday he smiles and gives 110 percent. I'm not pulling any plugs".

A nurse points to the 21 inch color television. A male news caster says. "Today in Teheran. Iranian students took over the United States embassy. 88 Americans were taken hostage. That's the way it is this November 4th 1979".

BAY VIEW HIGH SCHOOL GYM - DIMLY LIT - 1983

The Beat Boys play a different style of music. The band has aged. The dimly lit dance floor is filled. Some dancers hair is gray. Walley and Mary Ellen have aged 20 years.

BERLIN WALL - BRANDENBURG GATE - JUNE 12, 1987

President Reagan wears a black suit as he stands on stage. 45,000 German watch. "Mr. Gorbachev open this gate. Mr. Gorbachev tear down this wall". The crowd goes wild.

BAY VIEW HIGH SCHOOL GYM - DIMLY LIT - 1993

The Beat Boys have aged. They play their oldie but goodie songs from years gone bye. The dance floor is filled with middle aged heavier people. They stumble bumble to the same songs they twisted to 30 years ago. Walley Crawford and Mary Ellen blend into the crowd.

CHAPTER 15 - EDDIE GETS A WAKE UP CALL

SEPTEMBER 11, 2001 - NEW YORK CITY - MORNING
American Airlines Flight 11 leaving Boston is hijacked by five al-Qaeda terrorists. The Boeing 767-223ER airline carries 92 passengers and crew. It is deliberately crashed into the North Tower of the World Trade Center at 8:46, killing everyone aboard the flight and resulting in the deaths of more than one thousand.

United Airlines Flight 175 leaving Boston is hijacked by five al-Qaeda terrorists. The Boeing 767-200 carrying 65 passengers and crew at 9:03 is deliberately crashed into the South Tower of the World Trade Center, killing everyone aboard and causing the deaths of more than 600 people in the South Towers upper levels. The damage done to the South Tower by the crash and subsequent fire caused its collapse 56 minutes later at 9:59, killing everyone who was still inside. Heavy dense smoke fills the New York city air. People cry, people run, there is chaos in the streets.

At 10:28 that morning the North Tower collapses. Resulting in hundreds of additional causalities. On September 11, 2001, 2,977 people are killed. It's the deadliest terrorist attack in American history. America goes into shock. America mourns.

MAYO CLINIC - HOSPITAL ROOM - SEPTEMBER 11, 2001
All is peaceful and quiet except for the sound of a oxygen machine. Eddie lies in a coma. He breathes in rhythm on his machine, in and out in and out. No hospital staff present. Eddie is alone, very quiet very peaceful ....

Eddie hears. Whistling (Sweet Georgia Brown) Leroy Johnson appears. Eddie sits straight up, eyes wide open. Leroy Johnson points to the window. "You see what the Hell is going on out there. Thousands of Americans dead. You've jagged off on that treadmill long enough. Edward (Shape up get serious) Help us. Ask what you can do for your country". Leroy Johnson disappears. Eddie falls back into his coma.

MAYO CLINIC FITNESS ROOM - THAT AFTERNOON

Eddie's hair shows gray, as he steps on the treadmill. Two nurses strap Eddie to his harness. The bored staff looks on. Doctor Ben Casey yawns. "Okay nurse start the treadmill 2 mph". Eddie walks back straight, his arms swing. The staff looks. "Nurse increase the speed to 3.5 mph. Eddie walks, swings his arms. He cracks open his eyes a bit. The staff smiles.

Ben Casey looks. "Nurse increase to 4 mph". A janitor wipes the television. He turns on MTV, Rocky type music plays. "Getting stronger wont be long now". Eddie comfortably jogs. The janitor turns the music up. A crowd pours into the room. "Nurse increase to 5 mph. The crowd chants. "Go Eddie Go, Run Eddie run". Eddie runs. The Doctors look! The music plays. The crowd cheers. Ben Casey reacts. "I knew it. This guy is a fighter. He's on his way back. I wish the plug pullers could see Eddie now. Go Eddie go".

CHAPTER 16 - WELCOME TO 2023

BAY VIEW HIGH SCHOOL GYM - DIMLY LIT - SEPT 10, 2023
The dance floor is full. The Beat Boys stop playing. The bright lights turn on. The band has aged. The dancers are old and gray. Most men have lost hair. Everyone has gained weight. The large sign hanging on stage reads. BAY VIEW HIGH 60 YEAR CLASS REUNION

MAYO CLINIC - HOSPITAL ROOM - SEPTEMBER 11, 2023
Eddie wakes up, rubs his eyes. Eddie looks around. He sees his black prom suit hanging. Eddie smiles as he rips the cords from the machines off his fit body. He jumps out of bed. Eddie dresses into his black suit with the white shirt. He looks in the mirror. Eddie ties his black tie. "Ha ha fits like a glove". Eddie taps his back pocket, feels his wallet. Eddie grabs his bag of coins. Unties it, looks at the $18.36 check kisses it, puts it in his wallet. He creeps to the door, looks into the long hallway. He sees doctors, nurses, hospital staff, security guards. Eddie adjusts his tie as he steps into the hall. His black dress shoes clank as he walks quickly, hiding his face. A nurse at her desk looks up. "Eddie - Mr. Harper"?

The crowd stops, looks. Eddie Runs. A security 25 year old security guard, drinking a big gulp yells. "Hey you stop". Two young guards chase the sprinting 77 year old Eddie down the long hallway. People stop look. "Wow"! Eddie turns right, he flies up four flights of stairs. The young guards take the elevator. Eddie runs down long halls. People stop, watch Eddie run and run. He rambles down 6 flights of stairs. Eddie sees an exit door with a long horizontal brass handle down the long hallway. The guards huff, puff. Eddie flies towards that door. The young security guards hold their ribs, huff puff. They stop fall to the floor. Eddie arrives at the exit door. He places both hands on the long brass handle. Eddie slowly pushes open the large door.

(IN COLOR) - ROCHESTER MINNESOTA - CITY STREET

The bright morning sun pierces Eddie's eyes. He shades his face as he stares at a 300 pound 20 year old male. The man is dressed in long baggy shorts, an oversized untucked sloppy T-shirt. He wears an earring, with many tattoos on his fat body. The whale rolls down the city street as he gulps down a half gallon sized soda.

Eddie runs the Minnesota street. He sees tattoo parlors, strip clubs, massage parlors and marijuana dispensaries. He looks at all the small space ship type of cars with rude drivers, honking horns, showing each other the finger. Eddie slows to a walk. He notices people locking up their houses in broad daylight.

Eddie stops and rests on a bench. He adjusts his collar fixes his tie. Eddie notices high school girls walking to school, wearing short skirts. He sees boys shirts untucked with oversized pants hanging down. Eddie notices parents dress like their children.

A smiling stocky old black man (whistles) as he pushes a shopping cart. Eddie's eyes open wide. The black man puffs his cigar, tips his old tattered Milwaukee Braves cap. The old man stops. "Hey slick, I dig your threads. We've been waiting a long time for you". Eddie points at his chest. "Waiting for me? Dig my threads"? The smiling old man puffs his cigar. "Yeah slick that's a fancy suit you wear". Eddie tucks his shirt adjust his black suit coat. "Oh thanks sir".

"Yeah the last time I seen a suit like that". The old man spins, shakes and bakes. Eddie Stares! "The Beatles were on the Ed Sullivan Show". Eddie quizzes. "Beatles on Ed Sullivan? Oh you mean the Crickets". "No Beatles - You know the British Invasion". Eddie shakes his head. "Beatles - British Invasion"?

"Hey slick can you spare 5 dollars for a cup of coffee"? Eddie laughs. "Five dollars for a cup of coffee". "Yes slick, I promise to pay you back". Eddie opens his bag. He counts out ten shinny Franklin silver half dollars. "Here you go". The old mans eyes explode. "Wow slick thank you. I haven't seen money like this since the 1960's".

The old man sits next to Eddie, relights his cigar. "Slick your style of dress brings back fine memories for me. Back in the early 70's I wore suits tailored just right". The old man recounts, looks up toward the blue sky. "My just pressed flared pants, covered the bottom of my shank high heel shoes just right. Not dragging on the damn ground". The old man chuckles, puffs his cigar. "My starched paisley collard shirt with a sharp brimmed hat. Oh yeah, around the neighborhood I was called super sly".

The old man points to the people walking by. "Now look they wear wrinkled pants dragging on the ground. With a cheap ball cap turned sideways". Eddie shakes, puts his head in his hands. "Five dollars for a cup of coffee. Money since the 60's. Beatles? on Ed Sullivan. The British invasion? Memories from the 1970's. Where are we"? "Slick we are in good old Rochester Minnesota". Eddie reacts. "Minnesota, Milwaukee is not like this". The old man crosses his arms. "Man - It's like this. This is America baby".

Eddie grabs a newspaper from the old mans shopping cart. Eddie reads. "What the hell - it's 2023"? "Hell yeah it is. We've been waiting for you. Eddie you have work to do". Eddie quizzes, throws the newspaper. "How do I get to Milwaukee fast"? "Airport that way, one hour flight". "Where's a bank, cash my coins in"? The old man stands. "Bank you crazy? A bank wont give you shit for those coins". The old man points to a pawn shop. "Take your bag of silver across the street". Eddie runs to the pawn shop.

Eddie opens the heavy barred front door. The pawn shop is cluttered with everything but a kitchen sink. Eddie stops, looks at an 80 inch color television. The Jerry Zinger show plays, a fight between 2 scantly clad trans genders breaks out. A man behind the counter has a shaved head. "Hello sir can I help you". Eddie walks, rests his bag of coins on the counter. "Hi I have a plane to catch. I would like to cash these coins in for paper money". The man opens the bag of silver coins. His eyes fly open. Eddie studies the mans shaved head. "How much are you looking to get"? Eddie quizzes. "Whatever it adds up to. Count it up and pay me in paper bills please". The man looks at Eddie. He turns and yells. "Hey pa got a minute, you better come and take a look at this".

An eighty year old man with a full head of gray hair, cigarette in mouth strolls to the counter. He looks in the bag. His eyes go cross eyed. "Richard get me my magnifying glasses". Both men with specs, slowly inspect each coin. Eddie turns and watches Jerry Zinger. A Viagra commercial plays. Eddie looks! (mumbles) "What the hell". The men continue to study each coin. "Pa I see a lot of S's here". Eddie spins around. "Hey guys, what's the big deal? This aint rocket science. It's just change. Add it up and pay me in paper. I have a ticket to buy. A plane to catch". Pop inhales his cigarette. "Where did you get these? Benny Binion"! Eddie shakes his head. "His name was Ben Osmond, a paper boy back in 1963". Pop crushes his cigarette in the over filled ashtray.

"Will you take $500"? Eddie quizzes yells "500 DOLLARS"? "Okay okay I'll give you $600, but I'm not going any higher". "Deal - but cash this $18.36 check for me too". Eddie pulls a check out of his wallet. Eddie signs the check dated 4/26/1963 from Crystal Davis. Pop looks. "This 60 year old check is from Senator Randy Davis's mother". Rick grabs the check. "Oh boy we can frame this. Hang it on that wall". Eddie jerks, slaps his forehead. "Randy Davis is a senator. $600 for a bag of coins. Is this the twilight zone? Hey hey mark it paid gentlemen. I have a plane to catch and stewardesses to meet".

Rick and pop look at the confident Eddie combing his hair. Pop strikes a match, lights a cigarette, inhales, blows smoke. "When was the last time you flew"? "First time, I've heard all about the pretty stewardesses wearing their knock out white glove uniforms". Pop deals six crisp one hundred dollar bills. Eddie stuffs the bills in his shirt. He smiles as he struts out the door. Pop shakes his head. "Son I told you long ago. You never know who or what is going to walk through that front door".

CHAPTER 17 - FLY THE FRIENDLY SKIES

Eddie walks into the busy Rochester airport. He looks! The airport is filled with shabby dressed customers. He is pushed and shoved as he looks for a flight to Milwaukee. Eddie waits in a long line. He looks at customers dresses in oversized shorts and wrinkled T-shirts. Eddie notices the clerks behind the counter looking tired stressed.

A young female agent yells. "Next". Eddie smiles adjusts his tie struts to the counter. The female agent yawns. "Hello beautiful one way to Milwaukee please". She types, checks her computer. Eddie looks at her tattoos. "99 dollars and your drivers license". Eddie squints. "Honey, I just want to buy a ticket. I'm not going to drive the plane. Here's a C note, keep the change". Eddie pulls a crisp 100 dollar bill from his shirt pocket. "Sir I need some form of ID". Eddie jesters. "ID why I'm paying cash". "Sir do I have to call security". "Okay fine, no need to get all worked up darling". Eddie reaches in his back pocket. Pulls out his wallet. Hands her his drivers license. She Looks! Tosses it back. "Very funny, I'm calling my supervisor". Eddie waits, he turns, looks at the line of shabby dressed customers staring at something in their hand.

"Yes Page, you called". Eddie hears that voice. He spins back. He sees an older attractive woman. Her face is well made up. The pancake makeup foundation well blended. She sports a blonde bee-hive hairstyle with a half swept bang. Her fitted suit is well tailored. Eddie jerks he mumbles "Mrs. Crawford"?

Page grabs the drivers license. "Ms. Preston this man has a drivers license that expired in 1966". Eddie smiles. "Hello darling, love the hair. Do you own a beauty parlor, or are you just naturally creative"? Ms. Preston breaks a half smile. She checks out Eddie's fitted black suit. "I'll handle this Page. Go take another break or text your boyfriend again". Page walks. She pulls her phone from her purse.

Ms. Preston holds Eddie's drivers license. She clears her throat. "Mr. Harper", "Hey beautiful call me Eddie". "Eddie we have a problem with your license. It says you are 77. You look like you are maybe 50"? Eddie rests his elbow on the counter, looks into Ms. Preston's eyes, smiles. "I bet you say that to all the guys". "Not really look around". As she pulls on her white pearl necklace. Eddie leans closer. "Mrs. Crawford", Ms. Preston looks! Eddie jesters, I mean Ms. Preston. I've been in the Mayo Clinic a long time. I just want to go home". Her eyes explode, She bangs on the keyboard, hands Eddie a plane ticket and a note. "Give this note to security. If there's a problem have them call my office". Eddie smiles, taps the counter, "Thank you, have a major league day". "No Eddie thank you". "Ah for what", "We've waited a long time. Now get on that plane. You have work to do". Eddie shakes his head, jogs toward the gate.

Eddie moves through the airport. He stares at everyone and everything. He sees very casual dressed people staring at their left hand. Eddie stands in a long line at security. He watches upset customers getting their luggage torn apart and bodies searched.

A security guard yells. "Next, ID and ticket". Eddie hands the guard his ticket. "Stop where's your ID"? " Oh sorry, here you go". Eddie gives the guard his note. "Oh! Ms. Preston, go ahead next line". Eddie waits in another line. He looks and looks. A security guard yells. "Hey slick take your shoes off". Eddie points at his chest. "Who me, what why"? "Take your shoes off. Take your fancy jacket off. Put them in the basket, lets go". Eddie wobbles as he pulls of his shinny black shoes. He removes his suit jacket, stops looks at the metal detector. "Let go move". Eddie walks alarm sounds. "Hold it stop. Both arms in the air now". Eddie puzzled raises his arms. More security guards arrive grab Eddie. "Men take him. Scan him good".

A guard holds a lighted wand, he scans Eddie. The wand beeps lights flash. Eddie jumps. "Hey guys easy with that marshin thing". "Careful men frisk him". A guard pulls silver half dollars out of Eddie's pockets. "Explain to me why you have a one way ticket and no luggage". The first security guard waves a piece of paper. "Joe he has a note from Ms. Preston".

Eddie adjusts his shirt, tie as he struts on the airplane. He side steps casual dressed passengers jamming large bags into the overhead bins. Eddie flops into his seat, naps.......

An average looking lady, hair in ponytail wearing little makeup taps Eddie. "Sir put your seat in the upright position. Fasten your seatbelt". "Hello Ms. I need the stewardess please". "I'm your flight attendant sir". Eddie reacts. "You're the stewardess"? Her face flushes as she stares. "Can I help you"? "Yes a glass of water please". "That will be 5 dollars. Credit card only no cash". Eddie looks.

CHAPTER 18 - MY HOME TOWN ?

The plane lands at Billy Mitchell Field airport Milwaukee. Eddie high steps through the airport out the door. He looks round and round, up and down. Eddie's face wears the look of a tourist in a strange far away land. He shades his face from the bright afternoon sun, looking for a cab. A black cab, a 1957 Chevy stops. Driven by a woman in her sixties. Eddie smiles hops in.

Eddie looks at the thick glass behind the driver. She cracks open the glass door. "Fasten your seatbelt, lock your door". Eddie holds up his seatbelt, Stares. Eddie clears his throat. "Lock my door"? She shouts. "Yes lock it. Do you want to get car jacked". Eddie mumbles "car jacked". Eddie looks out the window. "Are we in Bay View"? "Yes this is Bay View. Where to"? Eddie boasts. 3015 south Delaware". She spins around. "Old town, are you a salesman"? "Salesman, why do you ask"? "You wear a suit on a plane and I'm sure you don't live on Delaware Avenue". Eddie's eyes are fixed as the cab cruises the streets of Eddie's boyhood adventures. "Sir sir do you live on Delaware Avenue"? "Ah - I used to - a while ago".

The black 1957 Chevy cab stops at a four way stop on KK Avenue. The driver pulls the heavy glass wide open. She extends her hand. "Hi my name is La Vern. La Vern Vitrano. "Hello sweet cakes I'm Eddie - Eddie Harper. They shake hands. La Vern pauses holds the hand shake. "Eddie seatbelt! You want a ticket"? La Vern reaches through the open glass, locks Eddie's door. "Trying to get us car jacked". "Car jacked - what's that"? La Vern laughs. "Ha Eddie - where you from Mayberry"?

La Vern drives. Eddie looks at closed businesses and small cars. "The chrome - where's the chrome"? La Vern adjusts her mirror. "What do you mean"? "The cars look like flying saucers in comic books". La Vern downshifts. "Yeah - Detroit is not what it used to be. Like here in Milwaukee. Most of the brewery jobs left town".

Eddie stares out the window of the black 57 Chevy. "Brewery jobs left Milwaukee"? "Yes sir. I had a great job". "What happened"? "The brewery moved, cheaper labor. Now I drive a cab. I don't mind. I meet all kinds of people". She looks into her rearview mirror. "Some are special".

The glass packs roar on the 57 Chevy as La Vern downshifts. She hangs a right onto Pryor Street. Eddie reacts. "Wow the old neighborhood". Eddie points. "I meet my girl in that alley right there". La Vern looks down the long shabby alley, shakes her head. She stops at a red stop sign. Eddie reaches down to tie his shinny black shoes.

SMASH - La Vern's window breaks. A greasy old man stabs La Vern, opens her door drags her onto Pryor street. He points the switch blade an inch from her frightened face. "Gimme your cash and cab Bitch"! Eddie bails out of the back seat. The old startled hood looks! Eddie kicks the mans hand. The knife flies. "Ouch you broke my freaking hand". Eddie connects with a left, then a right. The greaser goes down. Eddie grabs the mans leather jacket, pulls him up. Their eyes lock. The bleeding man shakes his head, wipes his black eye, looks! "You're - you're Eddie Harper". "Well well the Ferraro gang cursing Pryor street. Still up to the same old shit Joe". Joe wipes his bloody mouth. "I - we thought you were dead". Eddie throws Joe down. "I'm back".

Eddie attends to bleeding La Vern. Joe limps down the shabby alley. He looks back once, twice, three times. La Vern cries. "He knifed me good Eddie. There's a first aid kit in the trunk hurry". Eddie carries La Vern into the black 57 Chevy. "Get me to Saint Luke's hospital". He opens the trunk. Eddie shovels, pushes junk, moves a tool box, picks up a dirty white cowboy hat. Eddie stares.

"Eddie hurry up". Eddie tosses the hat, finds the first aid kit. He jumps into the cab. Eddie wraps La Vern's deep cut, stops the bleeding. La Vern smiles. "Nice job, you've done this before"? Eddie smiles looks at the Pryor street sign. "Eddie hurry the pain".

Eddie Revs the four barrel, eight cylinder, 327 Chevy engine. The engine misfires as it sputters down the road. "Damn sounds like this baby needs a full tune-up. Plugs, points, condenser, air filter, valve adjustment and some ethel gas". La Vern looks. "Ethel gas"?

Eddie speeds to Saint Luke's hospital emergency drop off. He jumps out, waves his arms. "Help we need a wheelchair". Two senior volunteers push a wheelchair, they cautiously remove La Vern from the 57 Chevy, place her in the wheelchair. La Vern grabs Eddie's arm. "Eddie" both seniors look! They run. "Eddie take the cab". "La Vern what are you talking about"? "It's for you Eddie, long story. Take it, you have work to do". "Gee thanks La Vern". Eddie spins the tires, burns rubber driving away.

CHAPTER 19 - MEET THE 2023 CRAWFORDS

Eddie dressed in his black suit cruises the streets of his hometown. He sees tattoo parlors, marijuana dispensaries. Eddie stops at a red light. Shabby dressed pedestrians walk by. Eddie checks them out. They stare, point at the 57 Chevy. Eddie downshifts as the black Chevy crawls by boarded up factories, where many of his childhood friends fathers worked.

He looks at the fuel gauge. "Damn it's on E". The black 57 Chevy pulls into a gas station. Eddie parks at a gas pump, turns the engine off. Eddie looks, Premium gas 5 dollars per gallon. Eddie looks squints his eyes. "Wow" Eddie waits.........

Five minutes later Eddie walks into the gas station. His eyes light up. The gas station is filled with aisles of fast food and beer. The clerk behind the counter wears casual street cloths, tattoos and a long earring. He jams to his phone as he texts.

Eddie stands at the counter waits. The clerk turns, texts. Eddie waits. The clerk jams. Eddie taps the clerk. "Hello". The clerk spins, pulls out his silver ear phones. Eddie points to his car. "Where are the gasoline attendants"? The clerk stops texting. "Gasoline attendants"? "I need someone to fill my car with ethel premium gas. Clean the windows, check my oil, tire pressure. You know, the usual stuff". The clerk tosses his phone. "Mr. suit, I don't put gas in your car, you do. The air you pay for. Check your own oil. Clean your own damn windows. You have plenty of nerve". He stares.

Eddie rips off his suit coat. "Okay fem boy". The clerk backs up. "Get me 5 quarts of 30w oil. An oil filter, 8 spark plugs, 8 new wires, a distributor cap, rotor. An air filter and 15 gallons of ethel gas". Eddie rips two one hundred dollar bills out of his shirt pocket. "Here's two C notes, keep the change". "Yes sir, right away sir".

Outside a crowd forms. Young and old watch Eddie tune the black 1957 Chevy. Like a master surgeon, the spark plugs go in and out with ease. Eddie notices the crowd building. He exaggerates every move. Eddie dances around the car. He moves like a Cheetah as he fills the tires, washes windows, removes the gas nozzle in perfect unison. He throws the tool box in the trunk, (pauses) looks at the white cowboy hat. Eddie waves to the crowd, peels out of the gas station. He smiles as the thrust throws him backwards. The crowd cheers roars. "Wow - did you see that! He tuned up that car without a computer"?

Eddie drives to his boyhood home. He studies the run down neighborhood as he parks in front of 3015 Delaware avenue. Eddie adjusts his coat and tie as he struts to the front door.

He knocks. A woman unlocks 3 locks. She cracks open the battered front door. Eddie smiles. "Good afternoon ma'am I'm Eddie". He extends his hand. She pushes the door leaving a one inch gap. "I used to live here. I'm looking for Viola or Jerry Harper. Do you". The woman yells. "No - no one here. You go". She slams the door. Locks three locks.

Eddie turns looks at his old neighborhood. No children play. He pauses. Eddie blinks a tear runs down his cheek as he enters the 57 Chevy. "Now I'm starting to get pissed off"'. Eddie fires up the four barrel carburetor. "Okay Crawford's here I come". Eddie punches the gas pedal. Tires spin, a cloud of smoke forms as he lays rubber all over Delaware avenue. An old man walking his poodle dog stares, smiles as he lights his pipe.

Driving Eddie looks at all the small cars, rude drivers. He turns onto Pine street. Eddie sees the street has changed. Pine street is quiet. "There it is 211". Eddie parks. He walks to the front door, rings the bell. Wally Crawford unlocks the front door. "No salesmen thank you". Wally pushes the door. Eddie holds the door. He stares. Wally has gained weight and his style of dress had changed to very casual. Eddie smiles, tears form. "Wally are you Looney? It's me Eddie". Wally looks. His knees buckle, they hug. "You're alive? Not a soul believed you would wake up. We thought you died". Eddie spins. "Heck I busted out early this morning. It's crazy Wally, like the twilight zone". "Come in come in, Mary Ellen, Eddie, Eddie's back".

They walk into Wally's middle class home. Eddie jerks, he sees two young boys playing a video game, on a large screen HD color television. Mary Ellen speeds into the living room. Eddie looks, her style has changed. She hugs Eddie. Tears run down smearing her eyeliner. "Eddie you look great. That black suit, Is that the suit you wore to"? "Yes it is". Eddie adjusts his tie. "I woke up, I looked, my suit was hanging like it was waiting for me. I said okay okay let's go we are out of here". Wally rubs his stomach. "Me fit into my high school cloths no way Jose". They laugh.

Mary's cell phone rings. She answers walks outside. Eddie examines the large high definition color television. "Wally whose rug rats"? "Our grandchildren, Todd is 11 and Tim's 9. "Boys say hello to an old friend of ours". The grandchildren stare at the video game. Wally pouts. "Things are different nowadays Eddie. It's not like when we grew up". "No shit Sherlock, I'm beginning to notice that".

Eddie holds his hair back with both hands. "Speaking of when we grew up. How's Candi doing"? Wally pauses. "Candi Candi - Oh Candi Midway. Last I heard she became an old maid. Candi never married". Walley answers his phone. Walks out of the room.

Eddie waits. He looks around. "Tim Todd what are you boys playing"? Todd stares at the video game. "Homerun derby". Eddie smiles. "Just up my alley boys. Get your ball bat and gloves. I'll hit you a few. They used to call me Eddie Mathews". Tim turns around. "Where outside"? "Brilliant deduction son. Your grandfather and I played ball in that same street all the time". The boys laugh, roll around the living room floor. "Ha ha mister you're funny. No one plays baseball in the street". Eddie looks. "Well than how about a game of catch in the front yard". "No it's to hot outside". "Yeah we play inside". "Tim I'm thirsty, lets get more soda".

The boys walk towards the kitchen. Eddie follows. He sees Walley and Mary looking at their phones. The boys grab two large plastic bottles of soda. Eddie stares at the large soda bottles. Eddie opens a cabinet, medication bottles fill the shelves. Eddie finds a glass. He fills it with tap water. The boys look. Eddie chugs it. "Ahh good to the last drop". Tim and Todd laugh, spill their soda. Their laughter continues. Mary and Walley enter. "Boys what's so funny"? "Grandpa your friend is weird". "Why's that"? "He drinks water from the sink, gross". Mary Ellen wipes the soda. "Boys go play your video game. Eddie please sit, we have a lot of catching up to do". With both hands the boys hold their soda bottles walking out of the kitchen.

Mary pours drinks. Eddie runs his hands across the same kitchen table he sat at 60 years earlier. Tears form in his eyes. "Wally where are my parents? What the heck happened to my house and the neighborhood"? Wally holds Eddie's wrist. "Sorry your mom died. Your dad sold the house. He moved to a veterans assisted living home". Eddie jerks. "Pa's alive! Where is this place"? Mary answers as she tops off Eddie's drink. "By the baseball stadium on Brett Favre way". Eddie reacts. "Who the hell is Brett Favre"? "He played quarterback for the Packers". Eddie smiles, shakes the ice cubes in his empty glass, "Dames and sports. "You mean Bart Starr". "No Eddie Brett Favre". Eddie throws his arms up. "Whatever - I know where the Braves stadium is. Got to go". Eddie runs for the door. Wally stands. "Eddie wait there is so much we want to tell you". "Thanks for the drinks guys. Maybe later - I have to go see my pa".

CHAPTER 20 - DADS ALIVE

Eddie wearing his black suit walks into the VA hospital. He eyes the receptionist. An older attractive blonde woman. Eddie smiles. "Hello darling, you look stunning this evening. I'm here to visit Jerry Harper. Would you be so kind to tell me what room Mr. Harper resides in"? She looks at Eddie's well fitted suit. "I'm sorry sir only immediate family can visit after 5pm". Eddie adjusts his tie. "That's me gorgeous, I'm his son". The stern receptionist breaks a smile, laughs and laughs. "His son? Ha nice try Mr. Salesman". Eddie jerks. "What try"? "Jerry Harper is 96 years old. You should of tried saying you were his grandson". Eddie throws his arms up. "Grandson I don't understand". She stands. "Mr. salesman you can make your sales call tomorrow, between the hours of 8am to 4pm. You will find Jerry Harper in room 505". She points. "Goodbye Sir". Eddie reacts. "Goodbye salesman? Hello Ms. I'm Jerry's son"! "Sure you are, show me some ID". Eddie reaches into the top pocket of his black suit jacket. Pulls his wallet, flashes his ID.

The receptionist looks at his Wisconsin drivers license. She stops. She slowly looks up at Eddie. Her eyes sweep up and down left and right. She faints. Eddie catches her fall. He yells. "Nurse nurse help she fainted". Two nurses run to Eddie. "Nurse where is room 505"? "Fifth floor to the right". Eddie runs. The nurses carry the blonde receptionist, lay her on a couch.

"Barbara Barb are you alright"? She slowly opens her eyes. He... "he's alive"! They look. "I'm sorry what did you say Ms. Midway". Barb sits up. Eddie... "Eddie's back"!

Eddie runs the stairs to the 5th floor. He trots the long hallway, looks in an open door. Eddie sees the large room filled with old veterans. Most carry canes, or use walkers. Some sit in wheelchairs. Most wear caps identifying the war they fought in. Some watch the large screen television. Some play cards. USA flags fill the room.

Eddie stands at attention, tightens his tie, stares wide eyed as he studies the massive room. His eyes lock on a man dealing cards. He wears a flannel shirt and WWII veteran ball cap that Eddie remembers so well. Eddie's eyes tear, as he walks past each staring veteran.

He stops behind his fathers wheelchair. The card players stop look at Eddie. Jerry Harper stops dealing. He slowly looks over his left shoulder. "My God - you're alive". "Dad" They hug, cry.

"Eddie forgive me. You were transferred to Minnesota. Then your mother died. Me and this damn chair, after 9/11 it got very difficult flying to visit. I'm sorry". Jerry cries. Eddie holds his dad. "Pa easy" "Son after 10 years, no one believed you would wake up. All the so called high paid experts said no chance". Eddie hugs. "I understand pa". Jerry looks at Eddie's eyes. "But I know your sprit, your drive. I knew Eddie, that before I left this earth you would come and visit me. My only son would not let me down". They cry.

"I got that sprit and drive from you Pa. The man that lost his legs fighting for our country. Never once pa did I hear you complain make excuses or feel sorry for yourself".

Jerry picks up a megaphone. "Fellow veterans I have an announcement. No one gave him a chance to live. But I knew his fight his sprit. Meet my only son Eddie". The smoke filled room erupts in applause. Many veterans rumble over to meet Eddie. "Son so much has happened since you left in the spring of 63. I don't know where to begin". Eddie pulls a chair. "Start from the beginning". They quit playing cards. Jerry orders pots of coffee and sandwiches. All attention is on WWII war hero Jerry Harper.

CHAPTER 21 - EDDIE MEETS COLONEL CONNIE BROWN

"President Kennedy was assassinated November 22, 1963" Eddie's head drops. "His dream came true, we put the first man on the moon". Eddie looks up. "Neil Armstrong July 20, 1969". Eddie stands, fist pumps "Hell yeah I knew we would do it". Jerry looks. ("Edward shape up get serious") 'Yes pa'. "We went to war with Vietnam from 1964 to 1975, 58,220 Americans died. Many badly wounded. Our boys went marching off to war. Well Son they aint marching anymore. Many are right here right now". The entire room stops, walk, limp, wheel to the card table. They grab a coffee join in.

The late afternoon turns to late night. Many veterans fill Eddie's brain on the last 60 years. From the assignation of President Kennedy to 9/11 to $5 a gallon for gasoline.

The early morning sunlight blasts through the windows. A haze of cigar smoke fills the large room. Empty coffee cups half bitten sandwiches everywhere. Veterans lie snore. Jerry continues to talk with Eddie. "That's about it son, the last 60 years in a nutshell. I'm sure you have noticed this country has changed". Eddie wears the face of a lost child in a strange land. He clears his throat swallows. "One more thing pa. How's Al Dawson doing"? Jerry makes eye contact with the awake veterans at the card table. "Al spent years in a POW camp. The Vietcong tortured the hell out of him. After the war, when prisoners were released, Al was never the same". Eddie jumps. "What do you mean"? He was addicted to pain pills. He lost his gas station. No one has seen or heard from Al in over 40 years". All the veterans at the table bow their heads. "I miss Al. We all do, what a shame".

An old veteran using a walker grabs Eddie's arm. Eddie feels the pain. "Son this country all we fought and died for is going down the darn drain. Our this country needs you. Edward please (Save the red Eagle)". Eddie releases the pain, looks at all the teary-eyed veterans staring at him.

An attractive middle aged female in full uniform, heels clank walks into the large smoke filled messy room. "Good morning gentlemen". Everyone wakes, sits up. "Well men from the looks of this room it was some party last night". Eddie check her out, whispers. "Who's that"? "Son that's Colonel Connie Brown". Eddie reacts. "A dame! Is a Colonel? In the Army". "Not so loud, she's okay". The veteran steadies his walker says. "She's better than some men officers".

Colonel Connie's heels clank as she struts to the card table. She holds Jerry's old feeble hand. "How's WWII veteran Jerry Harper doing this morning"? Jerry smiles looks up. "Oh pretty good for an old guy". "Ha ha and who's this fine well dressed gentleman"? This is Eddie - Eddie Harper my son". Eddie stands starts to salute. Connie grabs shakes Eddie's hand. "That's okay sir, we are all friends here". "It's a pleasure to meet you ma'am - ah Colonel". Connie does not release Eddie's hand. They make long eye contact. She squeezes Eddie's hand. "Have we meet before"? Eddie smiles. "Don't think so. I left town in 1963, way before you were born". Connie releases Eddie's hand. Adjusts her hair. "Thanks but I was born in 1955". Eddie looks. "What's your maiden name"? "Connie Brown I never married". Eddie rubs his forehead. "Brown Brown my boss back in the day always talked about a Sam Brown, helping him when his business was struggling".

Connie's face lights up. "Sam Brown my grandfather. Who was your boss"? "Al - Al Dawson". Connie grabs Eddie's arm. The entire room looks. "Al Dawson the war hero. You worked at Al's gas station. "I remember you the cocky gas attendant. You put gas in my grandmothers car all the time". Eddie spins points at his chest. "Yes that would be me". Eddie points at Connie. "Mrs. Brown you have a lovely granddaughter". Connie shakes. "That was my favorite song in 1971. Did you write that? Eddie smirks. Colonel Connie grabs Eddie's biceps. "You look great". She releases her firm grip. digs in her large purse. "Here's my card, I owe you a favor. Call me we'll have dinner". Colonel Connie's heels clank as struts out the room. The veterans turn watch her fabulous exit.

"Well gents I guess I have a lot of catching up to do". Eddie smirks adjusts his belt. "I'm sure you guys know what I mean". The room explodes in uncontrollable laughter. Jerry's cap falls to the ground. "Eddie thank you. We haven't laughed like that in a long time. I guess you still have it". "Pa I never lost it. I got to go see you men later. Get some sleep". Jerry wheels his chair chasing Eddie. "Son you can sleep here". Eddie turns. "No thanks pa. All those stories, all that coffee, I'll be up for days". Eddie runs down the stairs. He struts by the reception desk. Barb Midway stares. "Good morning gorgeous, you're looking good". Barb stumbles, gains control, dials her phone.

CHAPTER 22 - ELVIS BRINGS NEWS

Senator Randy Davis scrolls on his laptop. His eyebrows raise. Dials his office phone. "Marge my parents trust has a debit of $18.36. Call the bank check on it please. Did someone steal the account number"?

A few minutes later. "Senator" "Yes Marge". "A check for $18.36 dated April 25 1963 cashed yesterday". "April 1963? Who the hell cashed that check"? "It was signed by Ed - Eddie Harper". Senator Randy Davis drops the phone, falls on his chair. "Senator Senator are you alright"? "He's alive"?

Eddie hyped up on coffee burns rubber, drives away from the veterans hospital. He turns the knob on the car radio. Rap - Rap - Rap. Eddie turns the dial, he hears Spanish. He turns the dial, he hears screaming acid rock. Eddie turns the dial, he hears sad sad slow songs. Eddie turns the radio off. He stops at a long red light. Eddie waits.

He looks at the people walking, dressed in strange loose fitting casual cloths. Men wear earrings. Girls have multiple tattoos. People walking stare at their hands, bump into each other. Eddie shakes his head, laughs. "Damn this is nuts, I hope this is candid camera? If not, then this is one hell of a crazy dream".

The back door of Eddie's cab opens. Eddie checks his mirror. A sharp dressed man hops in. "Driver Milwaukee Arena, 400 west Kilbourn please". "Sorry sir, I know there is a taxi light on the roof of this fine 57 Chevy. But this is not a cab and I am not your driver. So why don't you make like a tree an leave". Eddie spins around. A man about 25 holds a guitar. Eddie rubs his eyes. "Elvis? You're Elvis Presley"! "Thank You Eddie, thank you very much". Eddie hits the gas. The Chevy barrels through the red light. Beep Beep Eddie swerves they make it through the intersection. "Heck Eddie you trying to get us killed. Hell I think I already died once". "Elvis am I dead"? "No Eddie you are very much alive".

"Elvis how do you know my name"? "Oh you're special Eddie. We watched over you from above. Many Americans have waited a long time for someone like you". "Elvis is this the twilight zone"? Elvis cracks a slight smile. "Ha it makes you wonder doesn't it? No Eddie this is it, America 2023". "My God Elvis, what happened to the USA"? Elvis stares out the window. "Eddie it's sad real sad". A tear builds in Elvis's eyes.

The out of sync traffic lights turns red. Eddie skids to a stop, into the cross walk. Elvis holds on. "Easy now Edward. You are alive for a purpose. People are counting on you. We took care of you for 60 years. Don't die on us now". Eddie's face forms a puzzle. "What ever"?

"Sorry Elvis, the timing of the traffic lights is way off. They can put a man on the moon". Elvis interrupts. "Back in 1969. Hell yeah! Just like JFK predicted". Eddie shakes his head. "Now in 2023 they can't get the traffic lights in sync. How lame is that"? "I know Eddie it's sad real sad". Casual dressed pedestrians walk past the black 1957 Chevy. Some look, point. Many stumble stare at the machine in their hand. "Eddie a band from England released a song in 1975. It's title (welcome to the machine)". Elvis shakes his head. "Wow I wonder how they knew"?

Eddie pounds the steering wheel. "Elvis look at them. Doesn't anyone care about appearance in 2023"? "I know Eddie it's sad real sad". Light turns green, Eddie drives looks. "The fast food joints Elvis. they're everywhere. Don't families have dinner at home in 2023"? "Few families have sit down dinners nowadays Eddie. It's sad real sad". "Elvis I remember my mother ironing cloths, cooking super". "Things are different now Eddie. Both parents have to work. It's sad real sad".

A driver on a cell phone zooms into Eddie's lane. Eddie swerves Beep Beep. "What the fuck"! The driver casually drives, talking on her phone. "Oh Eddie those damn phones are everywhere, movie theaters, church". Eddie reacts. "I don't get it Elvis. Are they all doctors? "What is so important"? Elvis laughs. "Beats me".

The 57 Chevy cruises. Elvis points. "Oh my look at all the drug stores. Business must be so good that their across the street from each other. They have drive thru pharmacies to go, wow. If people only knew". "Hell yeah Elvis, the Viagra commercials on television". Eddie holds his fist to his mouth. He talks to his fist like a microphone, using a deep voice. "If you experience an erection over 4 hours. Seek medical help immediately". They break into uncontrollable laughter. "Hell Eddie after 2 hours the mans partner would need a damn doctor". The laughter grows. Eddie stops at a red light. They slap five. "Oh Eddie thank you. I have not laughed like that for years".

"Elvis play me a song". "Eddie here, now"? "Play some rock and roll, just like you did on the Ed Sullivan show". "Oh those were the days Eddie. Now you're bringing back memories. Okay hell these red lights last 3 minutes".

Elvis grabs his guitar. He jumps on the roof of the 1957 black Chevy. He wears a sparkling sport coat, black pants, white shirt, skinny black tie, white socks, black shoes. Elvis stands adjusts his guitar. People stop look. Elvis rocks his guitar. Elvis sings. He dances. Elvis shakes and bakes with balance and control on the roof never missing a beat. Older woman faint. A man in a wheelchair rises, dances the twist. Young people put their phones down, clap along. Eddie yells. "Elvis you hound dog". The crowd roars. Elvis bows. "Thank you thank you very much". He hops in the Chevy. The light turns green. Eddie lays rubber. "Elvis the king". Elvis wipes his face with a white handkerchief. "Eddie it's been awhile, thanks man I needed that". The 57 Chevy cruises.

"Eddie I was sent here. There is something you must know". Eddie looks in the rear view mirror. "What's that Elvis"? "Al Dawson needs your help". Eddie downshifts. "What Al - Al Dawson is alive". "Just barely, Al needs a favor Eddie". The Chevy stops at a red light. "Where is he where's Al"? "After Vietnam Al was given the wrong medication. He was conned in a bad business deal. Al lost his gas station. With the wrong medication, people thought Al was crazy. The con artists put Al into a nursing home around 1978. They registered him under the alias name Allen Davidson. Al's money is running low. Eddie get Al out of there he's dying". Elvis writes, drops a slip of paper into the front seat. "Here's the address.

I remember Al back in 57 at Pan Pacific Arena. We shook hands. Eddie get Al out of there. They are counting on you brother. Don't let them down". Eddie reacts. "They who's they"? Eddie looks in his rear view mirror. The back seat is empty. Eddie fumbles finds, reads the paper. "That must be Oak Creek. No problem 40 minutes tops. Eddie burns rubber. Speeds south on Highway 32.

CHAPTER 23 - EDDIE WAKES AL DAWSON UP

NURSING HOME - PRIVATE ROOM

Al Dawson has aged. He lays in a dirty bed in an unkept room. Al has a swelling black eye. Medication bottles are everywhere. Two time war hero Al Dawson wears the look of a man waiting to die. "Water may I have some water please". Two heavy set armed orderlies walk into the room. "Quiet old man. Didn't we give you a glass of warm water yesterday"? The young big orderlies laugh. "Bubba fill that old cup in the bathroom sink. It's double medication time". "Good now this old codger won't hassle us all day".

The black 57 Chevy purrs around the parking lot. Eddie looks. "This must be it". Eddie sporting his black suit adjust his tie as he jogs to the front desk. The receptionist talks on her cell phone. She looks at Eddie, turns her back continues talking laughing.

Eddie waits. He turns, Eddie sees old men in wheelchairs staring into space. Most have USA flags mounted to their chairs. Eddie waits.

He reaches over the counter, grabs the receptionists cell phone. "Excuse me miss, it looks like you are very busy. Would you be so kind as to tell me what room Al Dawson is residing in"? The shocked frazzled receptionist, flips her long extension filled blonde hair. She grabs her phone back. She types her computer. "Sorry Al Dawson not registered here". She turns looks at her phone. Eddie yells. "Al Dawson is not here"? An old veteran wakes up, salutes the front desk. The receptionist yells. "Al Dawson is not here". Two medicated veterans wake up stand at attention. Eddie looks at his slip of paper. "I'm sorry hun I misspoke, try Allen Davidson". She types click click. Her eyes open wide. " Room 121, down the hall. He's never had a visitor"? "Well doll, I'm Eddie Harper pencil me in as the first".

Eddie runs. An older portly man wearing an Armani suit, Rolex watch stares at a clipboard. He walks out a room into the hall. Eddie plows him down. The clipboard flies. Eddie stops helps him to his feet. Their eyes lock. The overweight man limps to the reception desk. "What was all that ruckus about"? She puts her phone down. "I'm sorry Mr. Davis. That man is visiting Allen Davidson in room 121". "So why did you have to shout at each other. Dam it you know I have a hangover".

She looks at her computer. "First he asked for an Al Dawson". Butch Davis drops his clipboard. He whispers. "That man who barreled me over, like he plays for the Chicago Bears, asked about Al Dawson"? "Yes Mr. Davis he asked for him twice". "Who is that man"? He reaches over the desk shuffling papers looking. The receptionist opens a folder. "Ah he signed in as Eddie, Eddie Harper sir". "What" - He's alive"? Butch Davis faints.

Eddie slows to a jog, sees room 121, looks in. Al snores, Eddie smiles walks in. His smile turns to a frown. He sees Al's dirty cloths. A musty stench fills the small room. Al's bed sheets are stained. Bottles of medication fill his nightstand.

Eddie shakes Al. "Al, Al old buddy". Al's eyes slowly lift. "Don't hit me don't hit me". "Al - I'm Eddie remember me"? Al's eyes open. "Al Dawson - serial number N3794N. Careful soldier Vietcong everywhere". Eddie shakes Al. "It's not Vietnam it's America. "The gas station Al, remember Leroy. Al look remember me". Al looks into Eddie's eyes. "You're Eddie, Eddie Harper". "Yes I am, Al you remember". They hug and cry. "Eddie where the hell have you been? After you left us, the whole country went to shit". "I know Al I know. I see Al I see"!

"Eddie we thought, they told us you were dead"! "I'm alive Al and so are you". Al frowns. "Look at me I'm a mess. I'm always so tired". Eddie points at the door. "Al I'm going to get you out of here". Al breaks a slight smile. "It's not easy. Years ago when I was filled with piss and vinegar. I tried busting out many of times". Al touches his black eye. "To much security here Eddie. They beat me bloody time after time".

Eddie sits on Al's rancid bed. "Al remember when you would do 100 push-ups and 100 sit-ups everyday". Al breaks a smile. "Down at the Y they called me Al cast iron Gadaski". Eddie fist pumps. "Al start working out again. Quit taking all those sleeping pills. Al rubs his black eye. "What the hell is going on"? Eddie stands paces the room. "Get ready Al, I'm getting you out of this hell hole". Al stands limps to the door. "There's a lot more veterans held here". Eddie looks down the long hallway. He looks into Al's old eyes. "Tell them the reinforcements are coming". Eddie hugs Al, tears form.

Eddie runs down the hall, past the reception desk. Mr. Davis stares, Eddie winks, runs out the front door. Mr. Davis grabs his phone. "Get me Senator Randy Davis quick - it's Butch".

CHAPTER 24 - PRESS ONE FOR ENGLISH

Eddie speeds north to Milwaukee. He cruises 27th street. He see Leon's Drive-In. Eddie smiles. "Hell yeah the old stomping ground wow". He parks next to the old phone booth. Eddie pulls open the squeaky door walks in. He reaches into his black pants for change. Eddie looks at the carving in the counter. (DON MILLER APRIL 1963). Eddie pauses, stares. His eyes run up and down the battered neighborhood. Tears run down Eddie's cheeks.

Eddie pulls a business card from his black suit jacket. He dials he hears. "Thank you for calling the United States Army. (For English press 1) Eddie stares at the receiver held in his right hand. He hears the recording repeat again and again. Eddie looks at (DON MILLER APRIL 1963). He looks at the run down Leon's Drive-In. Eddie tears up, tension builds, the anger burns. He rips the phone down. Eddie Gashes, kicks the phone booth to pieces.

He straightens his tie tucks his shirt, walking to his 57 Chevy. The recording continues Eddie hears. "Press 1 for English, press 1 for English". Eddie burns rubber, drives east on Oklahoma avenue. He shakes his head, looks at all the changes. Eddie stops at Bay View beach. Relaxes on a park bench, gazes at lake Michigan.

A shabby dressed man wearing ear plugs, texting walks by. Eddie looks. "Hey bud can I use your phone"? The bum continues to text. Eddie pulls the mans ear plugs. "Sorry guy, This is one fancy transistor radio you have. I'm in a bid. Can I use your phone"? The puzzled man questions. "Transistor radio"? Eddie holds up two shinny silver half dollars. "Can I use your phone? It's a local call not long distance". "Wow sure thing boss". Eddie shows the man a business card. "Dial this number for me". Eddie sees the bums dirty hands and long finger nails. "It's ringing here you go boss". He hands Eddie the phone. Eddie wipes the phone with his free shirt sleeve.

Eddie hears the recording. (For English Press 1) Stress builds. Eddie punches number 1. The bum looks. A receptionist says. "Colonel Browns office". "Hello darling Colonel Brown please". "Yes sir, who may I say is calling"? "Eddie Harper dear". Colonel Connie Brown sits at a large desk in a beautiful office. World War II posters of General's Eisenhower and Mac Arthur cover the walls. Her intercom buzzes! "Colonel a Eddie Harper is on the line". Connie reacts - "Put him through". "Hello Colonel how are you"? "I'm fine Eddie. How are you"? "Oh doing pretty good for an old guy". "Ha - Eddie I'm so glad you called. Do me one favor please". "What's that Colonel"? "Call me Connie". "Sure thing. Speaking of favors". "What's that Eddie"? "I need one. Can we meet"? "Sure my office, the address is on my business card. I'll be waiting". Click "Hello Colonel hello Connie hello".

Connie grabs her purse. She fixes her hair and makeup. Eddie smiles. He fist pumps the bum. "Thanks guy. Wow a transistor radio that turns into a phone and a camera. I guess 2023 aint so bad". The bum shakes his head as he walks to his rusty old car. He dis-arms his alarm. BEEP BEEP Eddie jumps. The bum drives talks on his phone. Eddie looks. "What the hell". Eddie laughs. "I guess everyone rich or poor needs a car alarm and cell phone these days". Eddie looks at Colonel Connie's card. "West Silver Springs drive, south east to north west. 45 minutes tops".

He fires up his 57 black Chevy, speeds north on Lake Shore Drive. Eddie flips the radio dial. The light turns red. The Chevy stops at the crosswalk. Eddie punches the radio off. He watches the different type people walk by. Eddie hears a familiar sound. He looks to his right. A yellow 1932 Ford Coupe stops. The driver wears a white T-shirt with a pack of cigarettes rolled into his left sleeve. Eddie's face explodes. He jumps rolls down his right window. The yellow ford turns right on red. "Don ... Hey Miller". Eddie looks license plate FEB-359. "That's it February 3 1959. The day the music died, Don's car Don"!

The light turns green. Eddie signals tries to move into the right lane. BEEP BEEP cars behind Eddie blow their horns. No one let's Eddie in the right lane. Eddie lays rubber speeds straight, tires smoke. An attractive older woman waiting for the bus looks smiles. Eddie nods he feels 17 again. "Don this 57 cowboy Chevy is looking for you boy. Let's see if you adjusted your valves today". Eddie speed shifts. He blows by small foreign cars. He downshifts turns right lays rubber. People stop point. Eddie speeds by old men on lawn chairs. They rise wave. Eddie looks, no 1932 yellow coupe in sight. "Donnie boy, I have places to go and people to meet. I'll catch you later".

CHAPTER 25 - COLONEL CONNIE RETURNS A FAVOR

Eddie cruises to 4850 west Silver Springs drive. He parks. Eddie adjusts his tie combs his hair, walks to the receptionist. "Can I help you"? "Honey I have an appointment, Eddie Harper for Colonel Connie Brown". The receptionist eyes scope Eddie and his black suit. "Colonel Brown has been waiting for you sir. Down the hall to your right". She checks Eddie out as he walks the hall.

Eddie turns right walks. Connie smiles. Eddie looks at the World War II posters. Eddie swallows clears his throat. "The posters are they"? Connie stands. "When Al left for Vietnam he asked me to take care of them. I was honored. After my grandfather Sam Brown died. Al rarely charged my grandmother for anything". Eddie nods. "I remember the day we meet. The busted water pump". They share a long laugh.

A tear forms in Connie's eye. "Life is not fair. Al Dawson a two time war hero beaten tortured in a POW camp, he makes it home. Then goes missing in the U.S.A". Connie walks stands by the posters. "I took special care of these. I dreamed of the day, I would return them to Mr. Dawson". She hangs her head. "I guess it will just have to stay a dream". Eddie holds Connie's shoulder. "Connie a coach from U.C.L.A. once said. Don't give up on your dreams. Or they will give up on you".

Connie raises her head. "What do you mean"? "There's a man in a nursing home having his life savings sucked dry". "Eddie people get old and can't take care of themselves. They end up in a nursing home. It's tuff but that's how it goes". Eddie walks the room. "Oh Connie I know this man can take care of himself. He is beaten and over medicated". Eddie looks into Connie's eyes. "Colonel do you believe a two time war hero deserves to live in dirty cloths, a dirty bed pan and have bruises all over his body". Connie looks puzzled. "Two time war hero? Why isn't he at a veterans home with your father"? Eddie punches the wall. "Some scam artist changed his name to Allen Davidson". Connie looks. "So what's his real name"? "Al Dawson". Connie jumps. "What Al Dawson is alive"? "Yes Colonel right here on the outskirts of town". Connie grabs her purse. "Let's go". Eddie breaks a slight smile, rubs his fist, blocks the door.

"It's not that easy. Security is tight. They have 300 pound armed bouncers all over the damn place. Colonel, Al Dawson needs your help". Eddie looks into the Colonel's eyes. "Connie now Al needs a favor". Colonel Connie Brown stares at the posters. "You're right let me think about this. Colonel Connie sits at her large desk. "Eddie relax, have a cappuccino". "Cappuccino"? "Take your fancy suit off, Trust me you'll like it" Eddie smirks, rips off his jacket. "I'm talking about the cappuccino". Connie opens her closet, hands Eddie a robe. "Here change into this". Eddie looks. "Don't get any strange ideas. There's a shower in the back. I also have a one hour dry cleaners. Go shower. I'll get your suit cleaned and order some food too".

One hour later Eddie relaxes on the large leather couch. He is shower fresh and his black suit and white shirt are pressed military perfect. Eddie has finished off two cappuccino's, a latte and a large super salad. The Colonel puts down her pen, dials her desk phone.

"Get me Captain Jacobs immediately. Captain Jacobs enters. Eddie stands adjust his fresh pressed black tie. "Reporting for duty Colonel". Connie stands salutes. "At ease captain. I want you to run a mock rescue special forces training mission. Get me eight of your best men". "Yes Colonel". "Here is the situation. We have two time war hero Al Dawson held captive in a nursing home on the outskirts of town. C.I.A. agent Edward Harper will accompany you". Captain Jacobs shakes Eddie's hand. The Colonel approaches Captain Jacobs. "I want your men fully armed. I will also provide you with 2 M2 browing 50 caliber machine guns mounted on two jeeps". Captain Jacobs scratches his head. "50 calibers for a mock rescue training mission"? "Captain rescue Al Dawson at all costs". Captain Jacobs looks at Eddie. Eddie stares back. "All costs colonel"? "Yes captain avoid force unless it's necessary. Agent Harper will fill me in on your performance". The captain scratches his crew cut head with both hands. "Force if necessary Colonel"? "That's an order captain". Connie holds a salute. "Prepare for the rescue of war hero Al Dawson. Bring Al Dawson home. Do I make myself clear Captain"? He salutes. "Yes Colonel Brown crystal clear".

CHAPTER 26 - JFK PAYS EDDIE A VISIT

Eddie dressed in his fresh black suit cruises the streets of his home town. He turns the radio from station to station. In the distance a yellow 1932 ford coupe shifts into Eddie's lane. Eddie looks. "Miller you son of a bitch". Eddie floors the gas peddle. He blows his horn. The ford coupe blows through the yellow light. Eddie stops on red. "Damn" Eddie sees FEB-359. He pounds his steering wheel. The anger burns as he waits at the long red light.

A man dressed in a gray business suit wearing a large brimmed hat, hops into the back seat. "Driver take me to Woods veterans cemetery, 5000 west National avenue". Pissed off Eddie stares out the front window. "Sir this is not a cab and I am not your cab driver. So why don't you make like a tree and leave". Eddie shakes his head. "Boy oh boy I guess I should lock my car doors like all you characters do in 2023". Eddie waits, stares out the front window, he hears.

"Ask not what your country can do for you. Ask what you can do for your country". Eddie shakes. "What the hell"? He turns. The man smiles. "Eddie Chris says hello". "Chris! How do you know.."? The man removes his hat, rubs his right hand. "Chris has a hell of a handshake". Eddie freaks. "President Kennedy"! Eddie lays rubber, runs the red light Beep Beep. "Edward shape up. Trying to get us killed". "Sorry Sir, how do you know my name"? "Oh you're special Eddie. We watched over you. People have waited patiently for you". Eddie reacts?

"Eddie I'm pissed off at the way America is today. What happened to our great country? What the hell is going on in Washington? What the hell is going on at our southern border"? "Sir are we in the twilight zone"? "It makes you wonder Eddie doesn't it? Look around my God - oh my God". Eddie adjusts his rear view mirror. President Kennedy shakes. "It's like a bad dream Mr. President. Jobs moved overseas, the crime. People lock their doors during the day. Most cars have an alarm. The price of gasoline". President Kennedy jumps. "Hell there's plenty of oil.

The BP oil spill proved that". Eddie questions. "Oil spill when where"? "April 2010 off the coast, in the Gulf of Mexico. Sixty thousand barrels of oil per day gushed into the gulf". Eddie downshifts. "60,000 barrels per day, no way Mr. President". "Yes way, by July 12th they estimated four million nine hundred thousand barrels gushed into the ocean". Eddie slams the breaks stops at a red light. "4,900,000 barrels no way". "Yes way, get this Eddie. Finally around September 17th they stopped the gush. It is estimated that two hundred and ten million gallons of oil spilled into that water and that's only one oil well"! Eddie reacts. "210,000,000 gallons my God those poor fish". "But the kicker is Eddie". "What's the kicker sir"? "Not one politician, democrat or republican brought up the myth about the oil shortage. Oh yes the feared oil shortage that the American people were told about since the 1974 gas lines. "Why not sir". "Beats me Eddie, are they paid off by the oil companies? Only God knows".

The shit hit the fan when I left. Congress using hard earned tax payer money to bail out foreign countries and fund their wars. While hard working Americans fight inflation. Get tax increases every year. Gasoline prices increase every year. Don't get me started on the Warren Commission Report that's another can of worms". President Kennedy shakes. "What the HELL is going on in DC? I'm tempted to go there and kick some ass". Eddie nods.

"Mr. President things sure have changed. Beats me, seems no one cares that you have to lock up your house, set your car alarm. No one cares that in America in 2023. "You have to press 1 for English"! John Kennedy grabs Eddie's shoulders. "Eddie people do care! Many American's remember how it was. They just don't know what to do".

Eddie downshifts, the 327 Chevy hums. President Kennedy points to the pedestrians. "They remember unlocked houses, walking to school safely. The remember playing outside till the street lights went on. They remember good paying industry jobs right out of high school. They remember full service gasoline at fifty cents a gallon, before the so called oil shortage. I could go on and on. Eddie you remember how it was". Tears form in Eddie's eyes. "Yes sir I remember - I guess they will just have to stay memories".

President Kennedy pounds his fists. "Stay memories Bullshit. Eddie you should be dead. Why do you think you are here"? Eddie looks in his rearview mirror. "Ah - what do you mean sir"? "Eddie all these years we watched you, took care of you in that long coma for a reason. You're the one people have waited for and are counting on. It's time Eddie".

Eddie smirks laughs, points at himself. "I'm the one people are counting on, me? It's time. Time for what"? President Kennedy talks into Eddie's right ear. "To lead a massive march to Washington DC. No violence, talk to the elected politicians that work for the people face to face. Eddie smirks. "Massive march"? Eddie laughs. "Mr. President who do I look like freaking Moses". President Kennedy screams. "(Edward Shape up Get Serious). Look around, foreign cars, unemployment, inflation, gas over $5 a gallon. Car jackings, home invasions, my God". Eddie looks in the mirror. President Kennedy breaks down cries.

"Sir I'm sorry but it's 2023. I'm 77 years old. What can an old guy like me do"? President Kennedy rebounds, snaps at Eddie. "Old guy? 77 is just a number. Eddie you have the body and mind of a 44 year old. You were fed the best foods". President Kennedy points at the pedestrians. "While most of these guys ate fast foods. "We exercised you Eddie 12 hours every day. We feed you the best food for 60 fucking years".

Eddie reacts looks in the mirror. Runs his hand through his full head of salt and pepper hair. "You are right, I don't feel 77 years old". President Kennedy nods in agreement.

"Eddie you're the frog thrown into hot water. Americans have had the heat turned up gently since November 22 1963. They don't see what you see. They don't feel what you feel. Dam it Eddie wake them up"! Eddie stops at a red light. He slaps his forehead. "Now I get it. Sir I'm beginning to understand why I'm still here".

JFK points to the overweight sloppy dressed people walking, staring at the machine in their hand. "Look Eddie these are good American people. They mean well, it's not their fault. They're fed fast food, sugar and dumbed down". Eddie questions. "Dumbed down"? Eddie they have the same DNA as their relatives, the greatest generation. The ones who stormed Normandy and the beaches at Iwo Jima". Eddie questions. "DNA"? JFK makes a strong fist. "Same blood running through their veins". Eddie nods pumps his fist, smiles. "Right sir, inside they have the same fight, like their great great grandparents. The ones who stormed the beaches at Normandy and raised the flag at Iwo Jima".

Eddie asks. "Iwo Jima, sir do we still own that island"? JFK barks. "Hell no we gave it back in 1968. Another fuck up after I left. 6,800 Americans died 20,000 wounded. Arms blown off, legs cut in half. Taking that island cost many GI's their quality of life.". JFK sweats, stares out the window. "All for nothing, unbelievable". Iwo Jima would have been a great strategic port. Especially the way China's acting these days.

Light turns green. JFK continues. "People are counting on you Eddie. Many older Americans are hoping waiting praying. That someone like you shows up, lights a fire that. Wakes America up"! "Mr. President I'm one guy. How is that possible"? President Kennedy holds his heart, grabs Eddie's collar. "After that bloody World War II a large group made a pledge. If the USA turned into a wimp. A coward in the eyes of the other nations. If our mighty eagles face turns red! The code words (Save the red Eagle). Passed down through generations means. March to Washington DC now! Take care of business". Eddie reacts! Light turns green, Eddie punches the gas peddle. "Wow Mr. President now I get it. I have heard those four words many times by many veterans. Now I understand what they were saying". Eddie downshifts turns left onto National Avenue. The finely tuned American made 327 Chevy hums heads west.

Eddie turns right, They enter Woods Veterans Cemetery. Row after row of white tombstones fill Eddie's vision. Eddie and JFK exit the black 57 Chevy. They walk to the top of the hill overlooking the entire 51 acre cemetery. Thousands of tombstones glisten in the setting sun. President Kennedy kneels. "Eddie get your ass to Washington. Talk to the politicians face to face man to man. A government of the people by the people shall not parish from earth". Eddie hands on his head spins round and round.

"(Save the red Eagle) Now I get it. That's what they were taking about. Now I know what I have to do". JFK points left to right, right to left. Eddie kneels. "All they fought died for, Eddie tell them. They took prayer out of the schools. Tell them they took under God out of the pledge of allegiance. Tell them their great great grand children cannot say Merry Christmas"! President Kennedy cries so much his face is wet. "Eddie we are counting on you. Don't let us down. When you go on television tonight give them Hell. Wake the people up. Give America what it needs. A good kick in the ass. Say the four words many have waited a long long time to hear". Eddie stands salutes. "Save the red Eagle". JFK stands. "That's it, those four magic words will spark a fire in the hearts of many men and women. A burning desire that this country has not experienced since PEARL HARBOR".

CHAPTER 27 - EDDIE HITS NETWORK TELEVISION

Eddie wears his black suit white shirt and tie waits in the office of the television station. The newscaster a pretty 25 year old blue eyed blond, long legs wearing a short skirt struts in. The clanking sound of 4 inch heels breaks the silence. Eddie looks wakes up. This is Brittany Star. She sits facing Eddie, crosses her long legs. "Hello Mr. Harper. I'm Brittany Star. It's a short 5 minute interview. We will take about your 60 year coma. Any questions"? Eddie sits straight up. "Excuse me doll, you're the newscaster"? "Yeah" Eddie smiles. "Hey hey I guess it's my lucky day. I was expecting Walter Cronkite". Brittany looks puzzled. "Walter who sir"?

A senior business man enters the room. He smiles double shakes Eddie's hands. "Eddie this is quite an honor. My name is Marty Jensen, I run this station. We are going live tonight with CNN". Eddie adjusts his black tie. "Mr. Jensen it's my pleasure". "Eddie I always wanted to thank you". Eddie points at himself. "Thank me"? "Yes Eddie you. A long time ago walking to school, a bully always hassled me. "Oh I'm sorry to hear that sir". Marty's voice cracks. "Then one heavenly day you showed up. Man oh man you cleaned that bullies clock. That Butch guy never bothered me again". Eddie stands smiles. "You mean pudgy Butch Davis". "Yes" They slap five. Laughter fills the large room. Bored Brittany looks in her compact mirror.

Marty's laugh turns to a smile as he wipes tears from his eyes. "Yes those were the days. Good old Butch, you know his brother Randy Davis became a Senator". Eddie reacts. "Wow so it's true, Randy is a senator"! Marty whispers. "Shaky election. Many years ago his father juiced him in. Keep that under your hat. I didn't say that". Eddie jesters. "My lips are sealed".

Marty continues. "And Butch, hell his senator brother set him up, as head of a huge government funded nursing home". Eddie reacts. "Nursing home! Where"? "Outskirts of town in one of the southern suburbs". Eddie questions. "Oak Creek"! Marty nods. "Yes I believe that's where it is. Crooked place, They receive government funds. Then they overcharge patients, mostly veterans big". Eddie grabs his ribs, rubs his fists stares. Marty continues. "I'm sure Butch and Randy have their hands out. Keep that under your hat too. I didn't". Eddie interrupts. "I know you didn't say that".

Marty looks at the clock. "It's time. Brittany, Eddie I'll be in the back room". Eddie adjusts his suit jacket. Brittany flips her long blond hair. They sit look at the camera, "three two one". Brittany smiles. "Good evening I'm Brittany Star. With me is a man who was in a coma for 60 years. A day or two ago he woke up. We are honored to have the first interview. Here is Milwaukee's own, Eddie Harper"! Brittany and the small studio audience clap, Eddie smiles adjusts his posture.

"Thank You thank you, it's great to be back and a pleasure to be here". Brittany looks at her notes. "Mr. Harper you were in a deadly car accident in 1963. You woke up a few days ago 2023. That's 60 years. What's the biggest change you have seen"? Eddie adjusts his tie. "Wow! There have been so many dam changes, I don't know where to begin'?

Brittany turns a page. "Well sir is it true that in 1963, there were only about 3 to 5 channels on television"? Eddie thinks, counts on his fingers. "Lets see we had channel 4 (NBC) channel 6 (CBS) channel 12 (ABC) channel 10 (PBS) and my favorite good old channel 18 (UHF), with Dick the bruiser, his cousin the crusher and good old Vern Gagne". Eddie smiles. "Yes doll that sounds about right". Brittany flips her long blond hair. "Weird, only 5 channels on the whole television"? Eddie adjusts his posture. "Weird - why"? "OMG Mr. Harper, only 5 channels! How boring"!

Eddie sits straight up. "Not boring at all dear. As kids we played outside, rain snow or shine. We played tag, kick the can or we made up games to play". Brittany flips her hair laughs. "Made up games? Kick the what"? Eddie squirms in his seat. "Yes babe we used our imagination. We ran around outside till the street lights turned on". Brittany shakes her head. "OMG no video games. You had to make up imaginary games"! She puts down her notes. "Well as you can see everything is much better now".

"A few things maybe just a very few". Eddie adjusts his chair. "In my dreams I see the sights and hear the sounds of yesterday". Brittany crosses her arms. "Sir don't you like what you see. 2023 is much better than 1963". Eddie squirms points. "What I see is people locking their cars and houses in fear of being robbed". Brittany looks. "What I see is an oil spill in the gulf of Mexico. 60,000 barrels of oil lost each day. But the kicker is Brit. That oil well that spilled 60,000 barrels of oil per day for 4 months from April 20, 2010 to September 2010 never dried up, they had to cap it. But since the 1970's they tell the hard working American public there's an oil shortage. So gas prices continue to rise". Brittany thinks.

"What I see is a monopoly in the car insurance business". Brittany looks. "Monopoly"? "Yes doll, The politicians made law. If you don't have car insurance you can't drive. The insurance companies know this, so they all charge top dollar, even to perfect drivers. Remember when long distance calls cost a lot more". Brittany thinks.

"What I see is Congress sending billions of dollars in foreign aide. Then raising the taxes of the American people who voted them into office". I see politicians giving free money to illegal aliens, while Americans fight inflation and lose their place of residence". Brittany looks puzzled. "So to answer your question Ms. newscaster. I'm pissed off and disappointed at what I see today. What happened to our great country"?

Eddie jumps up points, looks into the camera. Brittany stands, pulls on her short skirt. "Mr. Harper"! "Fellow Americans, I know you're out there. You remember America how it used to be. I know you are pissed off. I'm pissed off too. Enough is enough. Today we the people take a stand. Today we the people take America back"!

Inside the control room, 12 televisions cover the walls. Eight people including boss Marty Jensen wear headphones work the room. The studio manager yells. "Go to commercial quick"! Marty intercepts. "No! If anyone goes to commercial your ass is fired. Zoom in on Eddie. I owe this man a favor. (I pay my debts").

Eddie loosens his tie paces the set. He stares into the camera, raises both arms. "Everyone get up, rise! Get your asses off the couch. Open your locked windows. Unlock your front doors. Shout I'm freaking pisses off. I'm marching to Washington DC now"! Brittany cries. "Mr. Harper please"!

Eddie picks up the pace he shakes and bakes. "Come on people, I can't hear you. I know you remember. America how it used to be. Everyone get up. Open the locked windows. Unlock your front doors shout". The studio audience stands shouts. "I'm freaking pissed off. I'm marching to DC".

Inside the control room, phones ring off the hook. The studio manager sweats. Marty Jensen looks, a half smile forms. The crew answers call after call. The Manager pleads to Mr. Jensen. "Sir he's been going on for over 5 minutes". "Give him all the time he needs, I believe he's earned it".

Eddie plows on. "To the many Americans out there. I know you have that special spirit. The fire that burns inside you. The anger that burns. For many of you that furnace has burned for a long time. The time has come. Today is the day". "Mr. Harper please"! Brittany's four inch heels clank as she runs off the set. "Today we the people wake up. Today we the people get our rears in gear. Today we the people march to Washington DC. Today we the people (Save the red Eagle)".

Inside the nursing home, Al Dawson sweats doing sit-ups. Cheers fill the complex. Al stops stares at Eddie on television.

Inside the veterans home, Jerry Harper and his buddies cheer Eddie on television.

Inside a South Dakota VFW Post. Veterans drink at the bar. All is silent as they watch Eddie's performance. "Today we (Save the red Eagle)". An old 5 star general spills his tap beer. "My God the day has finally come. Men let's go". The entire bar room heads for the door.

In the control room phones ring and ring. Marty Jensen yells. "What's the response"? A secretary smiles. "Sir they love Eddie, they want him back". A senior staff member rips off his headphones. "Boss, the last time our phones lit up like this, JFK was shot"! Marty nods, stares at the studio manager. "Run the Harper spot every hour on the hour, the entire weekend".

CHAPTER 28 - ROCKY GRAVES RETURNS THE FAVOR

The next day inside a California hospital. An old man lays hooked up to machines. He is dying. The room is filled with crying family, friends of all ages. Many bikers wear leather vests. On back reads (Rocky's Angels). Pastor Ryan lights candles. The crying grows as the Pastor prays the last rights for World War II veteran Rocky Graves. Rocky's son Bo whispers to his crying sister. "Pa's lived a long exciting life". She wipes her tears. "Bo did father say anything"? "Nothing important. The last couple days he just mumbled on and on about the good old days he spent in the army". Bo's sister breaks down......

A faint whistle sound hovers over the room. People look around. The whistling grows to the sound of (Sweet Georgia Brown). Leroy Johnson appears with a phone in hand. "Telephone call for Rocky. Call for Sergeant Rocky Graves. Long distance call from Milwaukee. Private Jerry Harper calling". The daughter cries. "No calls I said. Let dad rest in peace". Bo intercepts. "Sis dad was mumbling about some Private Jerry. Who saved his life at the battle of the bulge. Put the phone on speaker". Bo's daughter reluctantly agrees. "Go ahead sir, you have a few minutes".

"Private first class Jerry Harper reporting for duty sir". Rocky's eyes open wide. "Harper"? "Yes sir, how are you doing sarge"? Rocky smiles sits up, pulls off his oxygen mask. The blood pressure machine dings. The doctor looks. It reads 120 over 80 heartbeat 78 beats per minute. Rocky pulls off more tubes. "Harper you sure as hell took your time calling". "Rocky I need that favor. It's a big one. I understand if you". Rocky intercepts. The crowed room looks shocked. "Bullshit Harper - saving my life, you spent most of your life in a chair. I owe you a favor (I pay my debts). Now what do you need"?

"My son is planning a march to Washington DC. He needs support. I know you formed a motorcycle group out there in California". "Yes yes go on private". "Sarge can you get your motorcycle group to ride to Washington DC? We need numbers Rocky, large numbers. The time has come sarge to (Save the red Eagle)". "Harper consider it done. We will be there". "You too sir"? "Yes me too". "Thanks sarge". "No private thank you". Rocky jumps out of bed. "What's all this"? He blows out the candles. "Pastor Ryan I believe you are rushing things a bit". Women faint.

"Bo tune my bike. We are riding to DC". Bo Graves laughs. "Pa you are over 90 years old". "I'm not dead. I've been waiting for this a long time. Nothing is going to get in my way. Who's coming? Or is a 3,000 mile ride to tuff for you boys". A young tuff muscular biker reacts. Bo Graves Jr. yells. "Grand pa I'll get the word out. Rocky's last ride, be there or else". Pastor Ryan throws his arms to the sky. "It's a Miracle".

CHAPTER 29 - BEN MIDWAY RETURNS THE FAVOR

Jiffy trucking company, old Ben Midway uses his cane to direct his 18 wheeler truckers. Ben's phone rings. "Ben here". "Is this Ben Midway"? "Yes it is, who's this"? "Hello Ben It's Eddie". "Who"? "Eddie Harper". Ben sits down. "Eddie we thought, well many said pull the plug, he will never make it. They said you were dead"! Eddie boasts. "Well Ben they lied, I'm alive". "Oh my God Eddie, what's going on"?

"Well Ben I need that (favor)". "Sure Eddie what do you need"? "Ben it's time, Time to (Save the red Eagle). Many veterans want to march to Washington. Most are older with combat wounds. They can't make the entire walk. Ben we need transportation. Many trucks your trucks, to help transport these disabled veterans to Washington DC. Can I count on you Ben"? Ben Midway rises, stands at attention. "Yes you can Eddie. I'll send all my 18 wheelers to Washington DC. I will also call my good friend CW. He runs Mc Call trucking out west in Oregon. Hell Eddie I know CW, breaker breaker, he will send a god damn Convoy. The gas and payroll is on me". I owe you Eddie. (I pay my debts). "Thanks Ben". "No Eddie Harper, thank you".

CHAPTER 30 - AL DAWSON GETS OUT

That night in the suburb of Oak Creek. An old military truck follows two jeeps. The jeeps are mounted with M2 Browing 50 caliber machine guns. Each jeep carries 8 fully armed soldiers. Eddie rides with Captain Jacobs in the lead jeep. Outside the woods, the rear of a large building comes into focus. Eddie points, "That's it Captain. Al Dawson is in room 121". Captain Jacobs grabs his radio. "Men your mission, room 121 bring two time war hero Al Dawson home". "Yes sir".

The 3 vehicles stop. Eddie jumps out of the jeep. He adjusts his black suit jacket as he struts the quiet lobby of the nursing home. Old disabled veterans expecting another boring evening mill about in their walkers and wheelchairs. The receptionist's feet are up on the desk as she chats on her phone.

Eddie grabs her phone. "I'm taking Al Dawson home". Eddie throws her phone down the long hall. She screams. "My god my phone my phone. Mr. Davis come quick". Butch Davis races up the hallway. Receptionist cries points at Eddie. Butch Davis yells. "Call the police security stop him". Three large guards tackle Eddie. Eddie breaks free. The guards pull clubs from their belts. Butch Davis points a gun. The four men approach Eddie. Eddie raises his arms, smiles. "Is that all you boys got? I think you are going to need bigger guns". Butch Davis smirks. "Harper you are out manned and out gunned".

Eddie yells. "Captain Jacobs now"! Two jeeps smash the front door. Hungry soldiers armed with MK 47's run to Eddie. Old disabled veterans cheer. Butch and his guards run to the back door. Eddie points. "Al Dawson down that hall room 121". Eight young GI's run. An old veteran throws his walker at Butch. "Yee haw, the re-enforcements are here". Eddie and the armed GI's enter Al's room. Al Dawson jumps out of bed. "Eddie I watched you on television. I knew you would return, Men". The young soldiers stand at attention, salute Al Dawson. Eddie hugs Al, pushes. "Al let's go (save the red eagle)". Al stops.

"Hold on Eddie, this place is packed with veterans, many of them want to go too". Eddie brags holds both thumbs up. "Hey hey Al my man, I knew that. Look out the window see that big old Army truck from Vietnam". Dawson's eyes light up. "That's your truck Al. Drive all your buddies to Washington DC".

Captain Jacobs yells. "Men secure the area. Check every room ask if they want out. Help them into Al Dawson's truck, let's go". Al stops. "Wait Eddie there is one thing I always wanted to do". "What's that Al"? Al rips his sink off the wall, throws it through the window. Eddie smiles. "Al I knew you still had it". Eddie and Al jump through the smashed window.

The young GI's wheel carry happy veterans into Al's old army truck. Satisfied Captain Jacobs, Al Dawson and Eddie watch. Small town Oak Creek police cars zoom up. Butch Davis struts behind the sheriff, points at Eddie. "Sheriff arrest this man". Captain Jacobs intercepts. "Sheriff this is a federal matter. If you do not vacate the premises immediately". A GI cocks the M2 Browing machine gun mounted on the jeep. "I will consider you and your men a threat to the federal government and the accomplishment of my mission". Other hungry young soldiers cock their MK 47 machine guns. The timid sheriff and his deputies dive into their squad cars. Tires squeal, a fog forms rubber burns. The small town officers speed away.

Eddie smiles, waves his arms clears the air. "Al here's the keys. Take your men to DC. I'll see you there". Eddie grabs Butch by his expensive shirt collar. He stares into Butch's eyes. Eddie's memory builds, the anger that burns. He throws Butch to the concrete gutter. Eddie let's go of 60 years of frustration. His eyes go blank, as his pointed black dress shoes smash into Butches ribs over and over. "Ouch ouch you're hurting me". Eddie kneels on Butches mangled ribs. "Tell your brother Senator Randy Davis, Eddie Harper and a few thousand of his friends are coming".

Captain Jacobs helps the last smiling veteran into Al Dawson's truck. "Mission accomplished, men move out". A shook up Butch lays in the street. He grabs his ribs, watches two armed jeeps and a huge truck of cheering army veterans fade into the woods.

CHAPTER 31 - AL DAWSON LEADS THE MARCH

225 miles south of St. Louis. A large army truck zooms down the highway 55. The large sign mounted to the back reads - Washington DC or bust. The truck is filled with veterans. They sing songs and share army stories from long ago. A veteran yells. "Hey Al need a break I'll drive". Al boasts. "I'm okay. This old truck brings it all back. I drove this truck in Vietnam. I can't wait to get to Washington and talk to our politicians face to face". The passengers erupt. "Hell yeah Al let's go". Al smiles. "How you men doing"? "Just fine Al, it's so great to be on the road again. Out of that prison camp". Laughter

The truck sputters/chokes stops. "Hey Al are we out of gas"? Al looks. "We have half a tank, what the hell"? Al turns the key several times rev rev. "Is it the battery Al"? "Hell no we have plenty of juice, It sounds like". Al exits the truck. A few men follow. "Squeak" Al opens the hood. He shakes his head. "Thought so, the distributor moved. The damn timing is way off". A concerned vet holding his walker says. "Can you fix it Al"? Al rests his foot on the front bumper, wipes his forehead. "Hell without a timing light! No not me. Al slams the squeaky hood. He looks into the blue partly cloudy sky. "I once knew a man that could time any car or truck without a light. But that my friends was a much different time in a much different place".

More veterans stumble out of the stalled truck. "What should we do Al"? Al scratches his head, paces around the truck. He stares at the sign mounted to the back of his truck. Al rips down the sign - Washington DC or bust. Al holds the large banner. "Men we have waited a long time for this day. I know many of you believed this day was just a dream a fantasy, it would never come". A few men bow their heads, hide behind other vets. "Well dam it, Our country needs us again! All the veterans remember, most try to stand at attention. Save the red Eagle day is here. Is a stalled engine going to stop us"? "Hell no". Is anything going to stop us"? "Hell no"! The rejuvenated fired up veterans exit the truck. Al Dawson points east. "Let's go we march on to Washington".

CNN news. An attractive blond reports from east highway 50 outside of St. Louis. Al Dawson and his crew of 50 old veterans, creep by her on crutches and wheelchairs. "We have a developing story. The cry (Save the red Eagle) from these disabled veterans of wars past. Their goal march to Washington, talk to their elected officials, republicans and democrats. A few of them are WW II vets. Many of these veterans are disabled. Some have one arm one leg. So with their crutches, canes and wheelchairs, the excited veterans proudly march. They sing, hold signs - Washington DC or bust. Many sources believe that through social media, veterans of all ages, from all wars, all states are uniting to march to capitol hill".

Washington DC Senators Office - Randy Davis and his staff drink lattes, enjoy lunch, watch CNN. Senator Randy Davis dips his lobster in butter, points at the 72 inch television, laughs. "Ha look at that old fart with his walker. Those old codgers will never make it here. Relax staff workers - This is not December of 1941. Now days Americans are all talk no action".

SECONDS LATER - Quartzite Arizona - Highway 10 East - A blazing sun hits the pavement. In the distance a cloud of dust rises.

MUSIC UP - (BORN TO BE WILD)

Motorcycles roar. A very large group, speeds down the highway. Hundreds of muscular bikers with determination in their eyes move closer. An old biker, riding a chrome low ride chopper leads the pack. They hold signs - Washington DC or bust. The back of the bikers leather jackets reads - Rocky's Angels.

CHAPTER 32 - POPEYE RETURNS

Back in Milwaukee, Eddie dressed in his black suit cruises east on Oklahoma avenue. He sees a yellow 1932 ford coupe heading west. Eddie waves, blows his horn. "Hey Don". The ford continues. Eddie checks his rear view mirror FEB - 359. He stops waits to hang a U-turn, looks at the fuel gauge. "Damn she's on empty, cool there's Al's place". Eddie turns into the triangle lot. "What the flock"? He parks the black 57 Chevy next to an old battered white 1961 Corvette Stingray. Eddie stares at the Corvette. "Strange, like a memory from long ago. Same car? Parked next to the same gas pump in 1961. Needed ethel gas. Wow I just blew my mind".

Eddie trots into the gas station. He looks "What the" Al's gas station has changed. The garage where cars were repaired has converted to a fast food store. Gone are the days of the 8 ounce coke bottles. Soda is self served in big gulp 32 oz. to 64 oz. sizes. The aisles are lined with chips and giant size candy bars. All kinds of beer and wine fill the coolers. Eddie walks into the next room.

An older attractive blonde woman is harassed by two young male clerks. She cries. "Every time you overcharge my credit card". "Laughing" "That's our tip old lady. Take your Metamucil, get your old ass out of here". Eddie moves toward the counter. "Give the lady her money back". The cocky clerks laugh. " Mr. black suit who the hell are you"? "I'm Eddie, Eddie Harper". Candi Midway turns, looks! "Old man go screw yourself". Eddie reaches over the counter, throws the clerk through the window. Candi screams with joy. "Popeye"! The clerks brother holds a gun to Eddie's head. "Say your prayers, you die today". He cocks the gun. They hear whistling (Sweet Georgia Brown).

Leroy Johnson appears, holding a large baseball bat. "Say hello to my friend. A hammering Hank Aaron autographed Louisville slugger". The clerk looks! "Where the hell did you come from'? Leroy swings smashes the gun to pieces, breaks the clerks hand. The clerk dives through the smashed window. He pulls up his bleeding brother. "They told me strange things went on here long ago. Let's get the flock out of here". They stumble down Oklahoma avenue.

Eddie smiles. "Leroy my man. How did you get here"? Leroy lights his cigar, adjusts his Milwaukee Braves 1957 champions ball cap. "Oh - I get around". Eddie struts. "Leroy thanks, we had those punks. Candi here was ready to nail that gun dude smack in his balls. He would have been on rubber leg street. Hell ya what a freaking rumble". Leroy puffs his cigar. "I know you could take those greasers Eddie. Friends help friends. Remember Al's speech". They Laugh. Candi's big eyes stare. "Eddie's back"! She faints. Leroy steps on his cigar. "Eddie lets carry her to the long back bench seat of your 57 Chevy. She can rest there". They carry Candi outside into the black Chevy.

Leroy looks, reads regular gas $5 a gallon. "Look at that terrible sign Eddie. I'm changing the sign back to 29 cents a gallon". Eddie jumps. "Hell yeah Leroy, let's pump some gas like the old days".

The sighs read Gas 29.9 a gallon. Cars on Oklahoma Avenue screech to a halt. Long lines form at the gas pumps. Eddie pumps gas, washes windows. Leroy checks oil, fills tires. Customers smile, wave. An old lady walking her French poodle stops. She hails her arms to the sky. "Praise the lord, Leroy and Eddie are back at Al's triangle gas station".

Wally Crawford drives up. rolls down his window. Eddie smiles, pulls a brown rag from his back pocket, wipes his hands and says. "Where's the vespa sir"? Wally frowns. "Eddie last night on television, and now this! What the heck is wrong with you"? Eddie wipes Wally's front window. "Hey sam you coming to DC with us"? Wally pounds his steering wheel. "Are you nuts? Eddie if you would have worn your seatbelt that day, this never would have happened".

Eddie stops throws his rag. Walks to Wally's window. He looks into Wally's eyes. "Listen up sam. If I would have worn a seatbelt that day. I would have ended up like you. The frog that stayed in the slow boiling water. No thanks pal. I see what's going on here". Wally speeds away.

CHAPTER 33 - THE MARCH STALLS

Highway 10 East - Dawn - 30 miles west of Las Cruces, New Mexico. As the morning dust rises, Rocky's Angels lead the way. Close behind are many 18 wheelers packed with veterans. Cursing around the 18 wheelers are bikers young and old, from all western states, carrying USA flags.

At the Las Cruces city limits, overweight Sheriff Jim Bob, cigar in mouth. Blocks Highway 10 East with police cars. An eager deputy salutes. "Road block complete sheriff". Sheriff Jim Bob rolls his cigar in his mouth. "It will be a cold day in hell, before I let bikers speed through my Las Cruces county".

A buzzing sound rumbles over the horizon. The desert morning sun reflects off the highway pavement. In the distance a cloud of dust rises. A testosterone charged deputy points. "Sheriff look". Five lead bikers appear on top of the hill. They speed downward towards the roadblock. Sheriff Jim Bob puffs his cigar. "Five bikes is all they got". He spits. "Shit this will be a piece of cake". Beep Beep! A convoy of 18 wheelers appear over the horizon. Beep Beep! The bikers slide to the side. The convoy speed towards the roadblock. Sheriff Jim Bob swallows his cigar. "Holy shit"! Sheriff Jim Bob and his deputies dive off road into the mud. The convoy blasts the roadblock. The sheriff's cars fly tumble and roll. "Yee Haw" The truckers and bikers continue speeding east on highway 10.

All is quiet. Sheriff Jim Bob stands, wipes the mud off his big face. He calls his brother Sheriff Billy Bob in the next state. "Billy it's Jim, they just busted my roadblock. All my cars are fucked up. Be careful I never seen so many truckers and bikers in all my life". The portly Beaumont Sheriff cocks his shotgun, chews his tobacco. "Don't worry about me little brother. My men will blow their tires out". Sheriff Billy Bob spits, wipes his mouth with his free hand. "No one fucks with my little brother or Bacon County".

Busted up police cars litter Highway 10. More bikers and truckers have joined the march. They raise their fists as they pass by the wreckage. A female fox news reporter interviews a mean looking large muscular biker. "Sir what is this all about"? The biker shows the peace sign. "We want to meet the politicians. Talk to them face to face. Ask questions like. Who do you give billions of dollars in foreign aid when Americans need the money? Who do you change your mind once you are elected? Why is gasoline $5 a gallon? Hell it's a $1.50 in Egypt".

The attractive reporter asks. "Maybe Egypt has more oil than us". The biker laughs. "Ha we have plenty of oil. The BP blow up 2010 gulf of Mexico proved that. Also why do they allow the monopoly of car insurance companies? Ever since 2020 price gouging is everywhere. Etc. Etc". The reporter asks. "Why not call their office"? The biker's biceps expand as he laughs. "Call their office, you get some clerk that gives you a song and dance run around. We are fed up". The tuff looking biker stares into the camera. "We are coming to Washington DC to get answers".

Senator Randy Davis turns off Fox news. "That's it. I've had enough of this bull shit march". He pushes his intercom. "Marge I want the best. Get me A Company".

Dusk settles on Highway 10 a few miles west of Beaumont city limits. Overweight Sheriff Billy Bob hides in the brush, with his army of deputies. They are armed with high powered rifles. A buzzing sound breaks the silence, The pudgy sheriff looks through his binoculars. "Here come those son of a bitches. Deputies I want all of them taken prisoner. Every tire you see blast it". A deputy questions. "Motorcycles too sheriff:? "Yes they fucked with my kid brother". He cocks his rifle. "These rebels have no idea what their in for. Lets teach these radicals a lesson they will never forget".

All is silent, then a sound of thunder draws closer. In the distance over the horizon of the setting sun. A group of bikers and 18 wheelers draw closer. Billy Bob spits. "Hold your fire. Wait for my command". The relaxed convoy cruises through the 7pm peaceful desert air.

"Fire fire". 30 high powered rifles explode into the lead bikers and 18 wheelers. The ambush blows tires and gas tanks. Trucks flip burn, block the highway. Bikers flip crash into the stalled 18 wheelers. Highway 10 resembles a war zone. People scream in pain. Blood soaks Highway 10.

Sheriff Billy Bob screams. "Yee ha! No one messes with Bacon County". The sheriff trots to a laid out old bloody biker. Billy Bob kicks him. "Grandpa - what's your name"? The old biker rolls over. "Rocky - Rocky Graves".

"Deputies arrest everyone of them. Use the off road 18 wheelers as a jail". A deputy questions. "What about the other trucks sir" "That's my road block. Keep them right where they are". A truck driver pleads. "Sheriff call for help you have wounded men here". "Shut up, I'll get doctors when I'm good and ready". The testosterone driven deputies bully, handcuff bloody wounded veterans, push them into the 18 wheelers that ran off the road. Many capsized 18 wheelers block Highway 10 east. Sheriff Billy Bob brags. "Look at my homemade 18 wheeler road block. Let's see the next wave of radicals bust through that".

Handcuffed bleeding Rocky Graves crawls towards his son Bo. "Bo this is bad, it's time to pray. Pray with me son, please God send us an Angel. We need your help".

CHAPTER 34 - A BLAST FROM THE PAST

The next morning Highway 40 East, 150 miles south of Nashville. A large army has assembled on top of a steep hill. This is "A company" fortified with artillery, tanks, and heavy machine guns. 500 soldiers hold rifles, ready for battle. In charge is 75 year old General Sam Keller. Second in charge is senior Major Jim Dec. Both served in Vietnam. Captain Don Hill salutes both men. "Reporting for duty General". "At ease captain. Orders from Washington. Stop the damn march". "What's all the heavy metal for"? The General shakes his head. "Politicians on capital hill grow nervous". Captain Don breaks a slight smile. "Last I heard it's just a bunch of old bikers and hippies left over from the sixties sir". "I know captain, I don't like it. Our first tour, Major Jim Dec and I, Vietnam. That was a bitch. Now many years later. We are ordered to fight unarmed American radical's from the sixties". The general shakes his head, a tear forms. Our country has really changed. Hell it's time to retire".

Senior Major Jim Dec looks through binoculars. "The first wave, spotted down in the valley general". Captain Don questions. "First wave"? "Yes captain. Sources say the march is picking up momentum through social media. Each day the numbers grow". The General grabs the binoculars from Jim Dec's hands. He smirks. "This I have to see". Sam Keller holds the binoculars casually with one hand, smiling, he looks. The General's smile fades away. He holds the binoculars with two hands, spits, blinks his eyes, looks.

The general sees Americans young and old, black and white holding American flags. They sing and march towards him. He sees bikers young and old with old veterans hitching a ride. The general sees senior citizens and disabled veterans hitching rides with 18 wheelers. American flags fill the valley. The general fumbles for his handkerchief. He cleans his glasses. He pans the crowd. "Men this aint some far out 60's march. Hell there's all types of Americans down there". He zooms in and out. "I see veterans in full uniform pushing the wheelchairs of disabled men. Major I see marching, singing veterans with Korea and Vietnam ball caps. Damn Jim some are older than we are. They march in the heat while we sit up here on our fat asses. They all look so happy like it's their first day in the armed forces".

The revived general pans the crowd. He sees and old veteran in full uniform sweating struggling with his cane to make the steep hill. General Sam Keller focuses on the man's face. Sweat pours, Al Dawson wears a determined look in his eye. Sam Keller shakes. "Al - Al Dawson? Hey Jimmie Al Daws...." "BANG" Blood flies! Al Dawson is hit! Al Dawson fights, struggles to stay up. Al Dawson goes Down! The General screams! "Hold your fire, hold your fire"! Major Jim Dec grabs a GI. "What the freak'? "Sorry sir slipped". General Sam Keller screams! "Officer down! United States military officer down! Special forces agent Al Dawson down! Medic get me a gall damn medic"!

The 500 troops look shocked. A medic runs to the general. General Sam grabs the medic by his shirt collar. "Listen up - you have a two time war hero down. Do not let him die this way"! The medic speeds a jeep down the steep hill. General Sam looks through his binoculars. The march stopped. He cannot see Al Dawson. A circle has formed around Al. The General sees marchers remove their caps, kneel, cry.

General Sam Keller drops his binoculars. Turns around, opens his wallet. His senior fingers shake, stumble as he removes an old black and white picture. A young woman sporting a bee-hive hairdo holds a baby boy. Tears fall on the photograph. The general prays. "Our father who art in heaven".

Bloody Al lays unconscious. People scream people cry. The circle opens, medic arrives. He rips Al's army shirt, franticly feels for a pulse. The medic sweats. "My god the bullet went deep. I can't feel a pulse". The medic cries, veterans cry.

Whistling (Sweet Georgia Brown). Al's big old army truck drives up. Leroy Johnson hops out. "Hang in there boss I'm coming". Leroy removes his ball cap. He whistles, fans Al with his Milwaukee Braves 57 champs ball cap. Al Dawson sits up. The marchers cheer. "Hip hip hooray"! Al smiles. "Leroy where the hell did you come from"? "Oh boss I get around". Al looks. "My truck - I knew you would get it running".

The medic opens his bag. "Sir the bullet is lodged deep in your chest cavity. I have to dig it out, stitch you up". The Medic pulls a large needle. Al looks. "What the hell is that"? "Morphine sir for the pain". Al pushes the needle down. "Doctor I have places to go and people to meet. Please put your drugs away". The crowd cheers! The medics face resembles a jig saw puzzle. "Sir the pain, you are blown wide open". Leroy Johnson hands Al a half bottle of Old Harper whiskey. "Here you go boss. Just like the old days. After work at Leo's gin mill". Al chugs the whiskey down. "Ah good to the last drop. Leroy you're an (Angel). Doc let's go stitch me up. I have things to take care of".

The shocked medic pulls the bullet out. Stitches Al. Al jumps to his feet. "Hip hip hooray" The crowd cheers. They march. The medic points up the steep hill. "Mr. Dawson you better ride with me". Al points. "Thanks son but I prefer to march with my men. We're taking Pork Chop Hill today". The puzzled shocked medic drives up the hill.

"Boss one more thing". "Yes Leroy". "You have to take your march south to Beaumont Texas. Many brothers there held prisoner. Need help". "Okay Leroy after I take this hill, we will turn south to Texas. Take the tired marchers in my truck" "Sure thing boss". Al picks up his cane, waves to everyone. "Let's go men. We have work to do. Let's take this hill". The rejuvenated crowd tackles the steep hill.

General Sam Keller remains deep in thought. Major Jim Dec picks up the binoculars, pans the valley below. "Oh no! Dawson's coming" Jim Dec shakes. "God help us. Sam I think we pissed Mr. Dawson off". General Sam Keller turns around. "What"? "Al Dawson is coming. He's jogging double time straight for you and me". Major Jim fumbles the binoculars. The general grabs them, looks. "Well - I'll be a son of a bitch". He adjusts the binoculars. "Old soldiers never die. They just fight harder". The General smiles. "Hey Jimmie Al Dawson is here". The medic speeds up the hill. "General he's tuff. He's a mighty tuff old Vet". "We know private. Dam it believe me. We know".

The General adjusts his ear phone. He motions to the 500 troops. "Attention fall in, form two lines. Welcome your brothers and sisters" The eager troops form two perfect lines 20 feet apart. They stand at attention in a saluting position, waiting anxiously for the marchers, bikers, and truckers to arrive.

Beep Beep 18 wheel trucks blow horns wave, drive between the perfectly straight line of troops. Bikers with mounted flags wave. Some do wheelies passing through. The marchers with canes, some using crutches, others in wheelchairs wave and salute as they pass through the line. Bringing up the rear, the last one to walk through is Al Dawson. His army shirt is torn and bloodied. Jim Dec starts a single clap. Then the medic claps. Suddenly all 500 troops clap as Al Dawson head held high walks through.

At the end of the line standing, is saluting General Sam Keller and Major Jim Dec. The three men make long eye contact. They salute. The General nods. Al tips his cap. General Sam Keller and Jim Dec watch Al, cane in hand stumble into the distance. Jim Dec looks at Sam Keller. General Sam Keller clutches his cane, looks back.

He yells. "Captain prepare the men to march. Captain Don reacts. "Sir"? The General points his cane. "We are going to escort and protect those American citizens to Washington DC". The Captain questions. "DC! Sir that's hundreds of miles". The General yells. "What is this a freaking geography class. I know how far Washington is. "I see 60, 70 and 85 year old veterans in full uniform marching for days. Are you telling me your young troops can't make that march". The captain intercepts. "Men fall in, prepare to march". The general hops on Captain Don's jeep. "Are you coming too General"? "Yes is that a problem captain"? "No sir no problem at all"?

The General orders. "Major take the heavy artillery. Also two tanks, two helicopters and two fighter jets for air support". Major Jim Dec smiles. "Yes sir". Captain Don fires up the jeep. The 500 anxious troops prepare to march. General Sam points his cane. "Let's go. If anyone fucks with them, they will have to deal with me. I owe that man a favor, (I pay my Debts)".

MUSIC UP - (WE TAKE CARE OF OUR OWN - Bruce Springsteen)

Captain Don shouts. "Troops move out - double time". The fired up troops, heads held high march - sing. "Everywhere we go people want to know".

CHAPTER 35 - THE MARCH CONTINUES

Back on Highway 10 at Beaumont Texas it's early morning. Sheriff Billy Bob and his deputies guard the prisoners. Many need medical attention. All need food and water. Billy Bob's huge masterpiece of overturned 18 wheelers and high powered police cars, block east bound lanes of Highway 10. A deputized man near retirement age walks to Billy Bob. "Sheriff the prisoners need a doctor". Billy Bob chews his cigar. "Let them suffer. Get Jethro from the TV station down here to film them suffering. The next wave of radicals will think twice about marching through my county".

Very old prisoner Rocky Graves cries out. "Sheriff can you spare some water"? Billy Bob laughs. "Grandpa I thought you bikers in your leather jackets and colors were tuff. Rockys Angels! What the hell is that suppose to mean? You are nothing but a bunch of sissies". Handcuffed Bo Graves jumps up. "Sheriff my father is over 90 years old. He's a veteran of World War II". Sheriff Billy Bob rams the butt of his shotgun into Bo's forehead. Knocked out Bo crashes into the hard sundrenched ground. Rocky Graves screams. "Damn you sheriff, you will pay". Billy Bob laughs. "Grandpa what the freak are you going to do"? "We have friends we stick together". "Ha you and what army? Any of your friends pass through my county, they will end up like you. Bloody and beaten". His men laugh. "Deputies lets go have some of that homemade ice cold lemonade that Aunt B sent over".

A few hours roll on. The Texas sun blares. The prisoners are parched. The sheriff and deputies enjoy shaking the ice cubs in their large frosty glasses of lemonade.

In the distance a Buzzing sound hits the desert air. Bo Graves wakes up. "Pa hear that beautiful sound. The sound I've heard since I was a boy growing up in Fontana California. It's Harleys pa, music to my ears. hell yeah"! Blood soaked Bo Graves stands yells. "The Harley's are coming. The Harley's are coming". Rocky Graves sits up, raises his bloody handcuffed hands. "Brothers their here. God answered our prayers. The reinforcements are here". Cheers carry through the make shift jails of 18 wheelers. The wounded and handcuffed prisoners come to life.

Sheriff Billy Bob grabs two shotguns. "Damn radicals will never learn. Deputy just like before. Give the order, blow the bikers tires out. These bikers don't know what their in for. They will remember this day. The day they tried to pass through Bacon County".

The deputy looks through his binoculars. Heavy artillery jeeps, tanks, 500 marching armed soldiers fill his vision. He sees bikers and truckers moving on. Leroy Johnson drives Al's army truck filled with singing veterans. Al Dawson with young and old citizens march on. "Ah sheriff I think we are going to need a bigger gun". "What? Gimme those". Sheriff Billy Bob grabs the binoculars.

The sheriff sees a tank, then another tank. He sees heavy artillery. He sees General Sam Keller leading 500 armed soldiers. "What the flock"? General Sam Keller orders. "Up ahead clear that road block, rescue our prisoners". The tanks slowly raise their gun barrels, aim. Billy Bob throws his binoculars. "Son of a bitch, run for the hills". "Fighter jet fire, tank #1 fire, tank #2 fire". Direct hit massive explosion. 18 wheelers, cop cars fly high, tumble, explode, burn in mid air. A jet fighter swoops low, parallel with Highway 10, fires 2 missiles into the roadblock. More vehicles explode burn. The road is clear. Prisoners scream with joy. Billy Bob and his deputies hobble into the woods.

The marchers arrive at the prison trucks. General Sam Keller and his GI's release the prisoners. The medics help the prisoners. Food and water is plentiful. A muscular biker speeds to Rocky Graves and Bo. "Dad grandpa you okay"? Rocky smiles. "Oh - I've had worse days". "Pa it's all over social media and CNN. Thousands of bikers, truckers and everyday people are heading to Washington DC".

CHAPTER 36 - AL DAWSON HITS TOWN

This is small town USA. People young and old line highway 10 Main street. Flags are everywhere. It looks like the fourth of July. The popular mayor walks the sidewalk. He stops to talk to Vietnam war veteran Adam and his two great grandsons. The mayor grabs Adam by his shoulder.

"Adam don't get your hopes up. I don't think the march will make it to our town". "Why not mayor"? Adam raises a cane, points. "My two great-grandson's Elijah and Elliot are looking forward to it. They love parades". "I'm sorry Adam. Last I heard, Sheriff Billy Bob of Bacon county set up a massive road block. Hell no parade is going to break through that". Adam pushes both hands on his cane, stands. "Massive road block on Highway 10"? The mayor shakes his head. "Yes, he is also holding prisoners". Adam raises a cane. "Taking prisoners? It's their right to march. That's what we fought for. Mayor - what the hell is going on with this country"? The mayor drops his head. "I wonder sometimes too Adam - I wonder".

Elliot and Elijah sit on the curb. They hold an ice cream cone in one hand, flag in the opposite hand. Elliot stands points his flag. "Grandpa I hear music". The faint sound of a marching band appears. In the distance west of town over the horizon, a parade marches on. Elijah stands. "Look parade". People cheer!
MUSIC UP - (COMING TO AMERICA - NEIL DIAMOND)

A marching band dressed in full red and white uniform plays. Baton twirlers dressed in glitter outfits, flip and turn. Cheerleaders pom poms in hand dance and cheer. High school and Collage football teams hold American flags, march. 18 wheelers blow horns. Leroy Johnson driving Al's army truck is filled with waving disabled veterans. Rocky Graves leads Rocky's Angels through town. General Keller and his 500 singing troops march on. High powered tanks rumble on. Last but not least, Al Dawson and his nursing home buddies bring up the rear.

The entire town flocks to Main street. Citizens cheer the massive parade. They open their locked doors, hand out food and water.

At the towns VFW post, Korean war vets, Chet Buckley and Maynard Hansen enjoy a beer at the bar. Through the open door they watch the parade. Chet looks, rubs his wrinkled eyes. Chet strains his senior eyes, spits his beer. "What's wrong Chet, beer no good". Chet stands points. "Look it's Al. Al Dawson is here". Maynard stands looks. "Son of a bitch, old soldiers never die". Maynard shouts. "Men, Pork Chop Hill, Al Dawson is here". A divine shot of adrenaline hits every veteran. They jump, sprint catch the parade. The young female bartender faints.

Al Dawson wears a ripped bloody shirt. He proudly marches Main street, waving to the cheering crowd. Al hears Semper Fi. Al sees VFW veterans smiling waving their fists. Maynard Hansen shouts. "Al you son of a bitch". They line up shake hands with Al, tears flow. Al points his cane. "You men marching? It's about damn time we (Save the red Eagle)". Chet Buckley screams. "Hell yeah, let's go soldiers". They parade marches east out of town. Many citizens, young and old follow the march to Washington.

CHAPTER 37 - WASHINGTON YOU HAVE A PROBLEM

Senator Randy Davis rubs his sweaty hands, he watches CNN. An attractive female reporter speaks. The Senator turns up the volume. "A code - all over social media. (Save the red Eagle). As you see behind me. All types of Americans from all walks of life have joined the march. Ages from Korean war veterans to Generation X".

Five star General Joe Powell watches CNN. He flips channels, the march is everywhere. He rises from his large leather chair, slams his office door, rapidly dials the office phone.

Highway US 50 one hundred miles west of Washington DC is jammed. Marchers - all ages all races sing wave flags. Eddie Harper smiles. Candi's face glows as they cruise in his 57 black Chevy. A big old army truck filled with sing veterans blows its horn. Al Dawson, Leroy Johnson wave. Bikers truckers motor on. General Sam Keller and his marching men lead.

Ring Ring - General Sam Keller answers his phone. Five star General Joe Powell screams. "Sam what the hell is going on! Have you lost it"? General Sam replies. "No General, but many feel our country has. It's about damn time we find it again". Five star General Joe Powell spits as he screams. "What the hell do you mean soldier"? "Sir you ordered me to stop a march filled with veterans. Men who lost arms and legs fighting for our freedom".

General Joe Powell falls into his large leather chair. Lowers his voice, looks down. "Well Sam, Washington gave me the orders. I didn't realize it was our brothers". "Joe we go back a long way. Remember America Joe. Remember how it was, when you walked to and from school".

"Sir people are feed up. I believe it's my duty to escort them to our capitol. Court-martial me. I don't give a damn. But you tell those boys in the White House, we are coming"!

High strung nervous, Senator Randy Davis has called in the National Guard, 1,000 troops, most young and cocky protect the White House. A few dozen bikers and millennia's arrive early. They set up camp on the White House lawn. A few cocky troops decide to hassle a hippie biker. They handcuff him ask for his ID. They kick his bike, mirrors break as the Harley smashes to the ground. A Generation Y marcher steps in, she screams.

"The professionals are coming. The professionals are coming". The trooper looks as he tightens the grip on the handcuffs. "Professionals? You mean more long haired hippie bikers". The troops laugh. The marcher replies. "No, A Company is coming". The cocky troops laugh. "We don't need freaking A Company. We can handle your type people no problem, no problem at all".

They push the handcuffed biker, face first hits the ground. "Laughter" A Generation Z marcher pulls out her I Phone. "I believe you have the problem". She shows the video. A Company's jet fighters and tanks blowing away Sheriff Jim Bob's roadblock. The bloody handcuffed biker cheers. "Hell yeah, the professionals are coming boys! With heavy artillery and sharp shooters. I'm sure you weekend warriors can handle that type of people". Word spreads among the National Guard. They pack up, run.

Five star General Joe Powell paces his office. He opens a large photo album filled with black and white pictures. The General sits at his large desk. He turns page after page. He smiles, he frowns, The General stares into the mirror. He dials his office phone. "Washington you have a problem"! Senator Randy Davis sweats, his tie is lose. He watches the march on three different televisions.

"General Powell, I ordered you to stop the march. The National Guard walked. What the hell is going on"? The General slams shut his photo album. "The American public is fed up pissed off. This is their country as much as it's yours and mine. They have a right to march. They are marching straight to your door. Senator you have a problem". The Senator loosens his tie stutters. "I don't get it. I thought we had the people dumbed down. To busy with their I phones on social media like Tack Clock getting likes, always texting. General for Christ sake what the hell happened? Who woke the people up"!

CUT TO - EDDIE HARPER

He wears his black prom suit, standing on top of the black 1957 Chevy. Happy Candi Midway slowly drives on Highway US 50. They are sixty miles west of Washington DC. Eddie raises his fist, screams at the marchers. The marchers raise their fists, scream back. Out her side window Candi stares at the march. She raises her fist screams. "We are almost there". The black Chevy hits a pot hole.

Eddie flips. His head hits the roof. Eddie's body crashes onto Highway 50. He lays unconscious. Candi slams the peddle. Chevy stops. She runs to Eddie. Candi shakes Eddie. "Eddie Eddie wake up". Candi cries. Tears fall on Eddie. "Eddie wake up, please God".

CHAPTER 38 - A NIGHTMARE ON 27 TH STREET

(B LACK AND WHITE)
Saint Luke's Hospital - Room 222 - MAY 1963

Eddie lays in bed. A large bandage wrapped around his head. Friends and family fill the hospital room. Candi cries shakes Eddie. "Eddie wake up, Eddie Eddie". His eyes slowly open. Eddie looks around, rubs his eyes. "Where am I? You guys look so different. "Mom you're alive! Dad Candi you're young again". Eddie tries to sit up, grabs his ribs "Ouch, is this heaven"? Doctor Ben Casey studies Eddie. "Easy son, you were in a car accident. You have cracked ribs on both sides. You took a terrible blow to the head. You were out for 36 hours".

Eddie touches his forehead. "36 hours? That's it, what year is it"? Viola Harper holds Eddie's hand. "Son it's May 15th 1963". Eddie grabs his ribs, slowly sits up. Hugs his mom. "Is President Kennedy alive? Is Elvis alive"? Laughter fills the room. Wally smiles. "Eddie it's been 36 hours. You act like you've been out for 36 years". The room fills with happy laughter. Eddie smirks. "Close Wally close. Hey Al how much is gas today"? "Regular is around 29 cents and premium or ethel as some call it is around 34 cents a gallon". Al rubs his chin. "Come to think of it Eddie, we have not had a gas war recently". Eddie throws his pillow. "Hell yeah now I know we are back in 1963". Jerry Harper rolls his wheelchair towards Eddie. He grabs Eddie's wrist. "What are you talking about son, back in 1963? Heck we never left". Happy laughter fills hospital room 222.

"Dad I did. Hell I had a crazy dream. I dreamed I was in the future 2023 to be exact". Eddie shakes his head. "Wow the USA was so different". Chip Crawford yells. "Wow 2023! Were there spaceships Eddie? And all kinds of weird stuff that's in comic books". "It was weird for sure Chip. Gas was around 5 dollars a gallon". Leroy Johnson's eyes grow wide. He looks at Al Dawson. Leroy laughs. "What 5 dollars for just one gallon of gas"? Eddie nods. "Leroy get this, you pay 5 dollars a gallon. Then you pump the gas yourself. Then you pay for air, that you fill your tires with. If you need oil, you buy the oil inside. Then you add the quart to your crankcase. The gasoline attendants just sit behind the cash register. No customer service at all". Leroy stands . What happens if a lady is wearing a pretty dress on her way to church". Leroy shakes. "And she puts the oil in the radiator". Leroy twists, dances. The room explodes in laughter.

Doctors, nurses, patients, hospital staff look, walk in. Eddie enjoys the large audience. He rumbles on. "The gas stations are crazy in 2023. That is nothing compared to what you go through at the airports. Fly the friendly skies, ha what a joke that is". Leroy shakes and bakes. "Oh baby this is funny, funnier than the Ed Sullivan show. Eddie tell us more of this crazy dream you had. After the last 36 hours, we all need a good laugh".

"Get this everyone locks their cars and houses during the daytime. Even if their at home"! Al Dawson reacts. "During the daytime"? Eddie nods. "How do their kids come in after playing all day? How do neighbors stop by and visit"? "Beats me Al, that's how it was day or night". Viola Harper grabs Eddie's hand. "Oh my, I'm glad it was just a dream. I could never live like that"! Word spreads through Saint Luke's Hospital. People fill room 222. Eddie smiles, enjoys the audience. He picks up the pace.

Eddie laughs. "Get this you guys, most people had car alarms. I saw rusty junker cars with alarms. It's crazy, when someone sets their alarm it sounds like a damn blowing horn. So when I walked through a parking lot and heard the horns, hell I ran like Bob Mathis". The room erupts in laughter. Leroy twists and shakes. More people push into the room.

Al Dawson jesters. "People need car alarms and lock up their house during the daytime? Eddie you had one crazy dream". "Al get this. People paid over one dollar a gallon for drinking water". Al rubs his head. "A dollar a gallon for wa-ter? What happened did the Russians nuke our water supply"? "Hell no Al". Eddie points to the sink. "The water out of the faucet was just fine. Just like the water here. But most people walked around with a plastic bottle of water. Like it's cool, like their hip". Jerry Harper looks. "Wow paying money just to drink water. Son that is a crazy dream".

"Get this pa. Here in Milwaukee in the year 2023. When you call a Government office like the DMV. If you want to speak English, you have to dial number 1". Leroy explodes. "What! Dial 1 to speak English in America? What the hell are we speaking in 2023? Did the Russians take over? Harper that's not a bad dream. Eddie you had one hell of a nightmare"! Laughter fills the room. Leroy shakes and bakes.

Eddie's smile fades. "Ah speaking of nightmares guys. Ah our president". Laughter stops, you can hear a pin drop, everyone looks. Jerry Harper removes his World War II cap. Al Dawson stands at attention. "President Kennedy! What happened to our president"?

"Eddie Eddie" - Smiling doctor Richard Kaye bursts into the room. Holding his chart he pushes through the large crowd. "Your tests are negative, no concussion that's a miracle. We checked 3 times". Doctor Richard removes the bandage. "Also your shattered ribs are healing quick, another miracle. We taped your ribs with waterproof tape. Go home". The crowd cheers! Eddie smiles. "I'm starved who's buying"?

A glowing Jerry Harper wheels towards the door. "Let's celebrate at Leon's Drive Inn. 3 cheers for Eddie. "Hip hip hooray, hip hip hooray, hip hip hooray". Eddie bows his head. "Dad I need a shower, give me 20 minutes". The cheering smiling crowd rushes for the door.

CHAPTER 39 - SANDY KOUFAX IS IN TOWN

All is quiet. Eddie gingerly walks to the a joining bathroom. He looks at his peacefully hanging black prom suit. Eddie sees his bag of silver coins, opens it. "Cool everything is here". Eddie smiles. "Wow Crawford's $18.36 check". Eddie looks in the mirror. He touches his face, runs fingers through his blonde hair. "Weird it all seemed so real, but no gray hair, far out".

Eddie turns on the shower. He closes his eyes as the warm water pulsates down the back of his neck. A peaceful divine light hovers through room 222. The crucifix on the wall moves. Whistling (Sweet Georgia Brown) Eddie grabs a towel, slides open the white plastic shower curtain. Leroy Johnson appears, wearing different cloths. Holding an unlit cigar. "Slick I owe you 5 dollars. (I pay my Debts)".

Leroy places ten Kennedy copper half dollars next to Eddie's bag of silver coins. Eddie grabs the coins dated 2023. Eddie flips. "Leroy I knew it! How the hell did you"? "Oh Eddie I get around". Eddie quickly towels dry, grabs his black suit. "Leroy are you an angel"? "Ha ha ha" - Leroy's pearl white teeth glow. "Eddie's back, what are you going to do about it"?

Tears form in Eddie's eyes. Eddie is lost for words shrugs his shoulders. Leroy puts his arm around Eddie. "Hear that crowd outside. They left the prom dance Saturday night. Waited for you, in the rain all weekend". "Eddie Eddie Eddie Eddie"!

"Son don't worry about the future. Hey it's the spring of 1963. Baseball is king. Sandy Koufax and the LA Dodgers are in town. Hammering Hank Aaron and Eddie Mathews are waiting". The chant grows. "Eddie Eddie Eddie"! "Come on Eddie - Let's go home".

They walk out room 222. Leroy puts his arm on Eddie's shoulder. Hospital staff see them slowly fade down the long white hallway.

MUSIC UP - (GOD BLESS THE USA - Lee Greenwood)
THE END

About the Author

As a young lad growing up in Milwaukee Wisconsin. I have never erased the two memories of. The Milwaukee Braves leaving town and Lew Alcindor asking to be traded.